Praise for

The Wishkeeper's Apprentice

"A heart-warming story full of wonder and magic.
It is brilliantly imaginative and utterly charming."

Abi Elphinstone

"A fun and original adventure with a zing of magic
all the way through. A wondrous story."

L.D. Lapinski

"Supremely charming.
I would've wished for this book as a kid!"

Carlie Sorosiak

"Imaginative, heart-warming… A magical tale."

A.F. Steadman

FOR Daniel, who has wished with me
from the very start.
R.C.K.

FOR Anna and Jenny,
my own strange magical accomplices.
R.S.

First published in Great Britain 2023 by Walker Books Ltd
87 Vauxhall Walk, London SE11 5HJ

2 4 6 8 10 9 7 5 3 1

Text © 2023 Rachel Chivers Khoo
Illustrations © 2023 Rachel Sanson

The right of Rachel Chivers Khoo and Rachel Sanson to be identified
as author and illustrator respectively has been asserted in
accordance with the Copyright, Designs and Patents Act 1988

This book has been typeset in Berkeley Oldstyle Book

Printed and bound by CPI Group (UK) Ltd, Croydon CR0 4YY

British Library Cataloguing in Publication Data: a catalogue record
for this book is available from the British Library

ISBN 978-1-5295-0790-4

www.walker.co.uk

THE WISHKEEPER'S APPRENTICE

RACHEL CHIVERS KHOO

Illustrated by Rachel Sanson

WALKER
BOOKS

The Comeuppance of Rupus Beewinkle

Rupus Beewinkle's years of exuberance were finally catching up with him. All the old twinkle and fun had faded away from his grey-green eyes.

The elderly wishkeeper had quite simply taken on too many wishes.

Rupus was hunched over a desk in his front room, stroking his long white whiskers and gazing without enthusiasm at the heavy files before him. He knew that he ought to make a careful note of each new wish snag in his records. But there were hundreds of them, and more and more occurred every day.

Each new wish snag felt like a brick tumbling down on top of him.

His life's work was crumbling into ruin. He had neither the time nor the energy to deal with the snags, let alone record them. Now, more than ever, he needed assistance.

As if on cue, a soft humming noise filled the room.

Rupus raised his weary head to look at the dusty wishofax machine as it flashed amber and swallowed a scroll of paper. He got to his feet and crossed the room to hover hopefully over the paper as it re-emerged, little by little.

A message, written in wet black ink, came out of the wishofax. Rupus sighed as he read it and his mood sunk even lower.

Dear Rupus,

It is with regret that we cannot fulfil your request for an apprentice. The Council has not received wishkeeping files from you for over two decades. Nor have any updates been received in relation to wish snags or other wish maintenance carried out.

The Council urges you to bring your records up to date. Once that is done, the Council would be happy to reconsider your application for an apprentice.

Yours sincerely,

Benjamin Tumble

Communications Manager
The Council of the Wishkeepers

Rupus began to speak aloud to himself (as wishkeepers often do). "Fiddlesticks! I should have known better. You can't ignore the rules for ever." He raised a hand to his wrinkled forehead. "Ah, foolishness. Reckless youth. Look at me now."

Rupus cast a glance at the wishfulness gauge in the corner of the room. It was tall and wooden and resembled a grandfather clock, except that, instead of a clock face, it held a single dial. Its golden arrow was pointing at a label titled *Downcast & Disheartened*.

"Worse and worse and worse each day," Rupus muttered, shaking his head in disbelief. "These wishes are snagging faster than I can keep up with them. I'm an old man who has learned his lesson the hard way."

Rupus closed his eyes for a moment. Then he opened them again at the sound of a quiet *pop* from the room next door.

Another wish had arrived.

Rupus sighed again. Then he made his way to the kitchen and saw that a small envelope was peeping out of his toaster. He carefully unfolded the wish card inside it.

"My, my, is he ten years old already?" Rupus murmured as he read the wish card, before cutting himself a thick slice of bread. He drummed his fingertips on the worktop as he waited for his toast. "It's no good," he mused. "I can't possibly take on any more wishes, especially not a Grade Four wish. It would be irresponsible. I already have over three hundred and forty wish snags to deal with. Seventy-nine of those are urgent. Twenty-three are nearly beyond repair. And the whole reason I am in this mess is because I've granted too many wishes."

He slathered his toast with lashings of blackberry jam. Then he hid the wish card inside an empty biscuit tin in the hope that he would forget all about it.

Rupus only made it as far as the hallway. "But that poor boy... And I do have some responsibility. Oh, fiddlesticks!" Rupus stuffed the last morsel of toast into his mouth. "I suppose I'd better go and check he's all right."

Felix Jones's Wish

Felix Jones adjusted the hood on his raincoat as he trudged across the gloomy sports ground at Whittlestone Primary. His worn-out football boots squelched with every step. In the distance, he could hear the excited chatter of his teammates as they talked about the football game they'd just played. No one talked to him.

Felix had joined the team last term with his best friend, Max. But now Max had moved out of town and Felix was pretty much on his own. He barely knew any of the other boys. Most of them were in the year above him and all of them were taller than Felix.

Worst of all, he hadn't contributed a single goal all term. Apart from the own goal he'd scored this afternoon. Felix winced at the memory.

A trickle of rain ran down his neck and seeped into his already damp shirt. There was no sign of his sister Rebecca's yellow Volvo in the car park. He checked his watch: 17:37. Of course she was late to collect him. That was *if* she'd even remembered to come in the first place.

It would be getting dark soon. Felix shivered. He had the uneasy feeling that someone was watching him and turned to check nobody was behind him. The field was empty, but still he couldn't shake off his growing sense of unease. It wasn't just today. He'd had the feeling for weeks, even before Max had gone.

Looking for a distraction, Felix headed to the car park's rusty vending machine. He dug out a pound coin from the bottom of his sports bag and slotted it into the machine before punching in the code for a peanut-butter snack bar. The shiny wrapper wound its way forward and stopped. His snack was stuck halfway down the machine, between the glass and a particularly plump bag of crisps. Just his luck. And the machine had swallowed his pound. There was a clink as a penny landed in the change box.

Things really weren't going his way today.

He retrieved the penny of change and stared at the empty car park again. There was still no sign of Rebecca's car. She was probably out with her friends and had forgotten all about him. She wasn't interested in spending time with him these days.

With a resigned sigh, Felix swapped his football boots for trainers and began a steady trudge homewards. His eyes remained glued to the pavement, counting puddles out of boredom, until he reached the centre of town.

In the market square, Felix finally lifted his gaze. Whittlestone's wish fountain stood proudly in place, surrounded on four sides by merry shopfronts and cafes. A host of copper pennies shone below the rippling water, twinkling under the warm light of the streetlamps. Felix's sense of unease dissipated. It had finally stopped raining. He paused by the fountain and reached into his pocket, remembering his penny of change.

Felix knew that magical things didn't happen to people like him. He'd walked past this particular fountain thousands of times before without any thought of making a wish. But something about this evening felt different. Besides, a penny wasn't worth much. Felix stared at the copper coin in his palm. In that moment, to his surprise, he knew exactly what to wish for.

Why not? It had to be worth a shot. Felix held his breath as he dropped his penny into the water.

3

The Penny Fisherman

The surface of the water continued to ripple as Felix's penny settled at the bottom of the fountain. He watched it for a couple of seconds but nothing else happened. He wasn't sure why he was expecting it to. He rubbed his cold hands and looked up at the warm glow of the bakery across the square. Row upon row of cinnamon buns shone in its window.

Felix felt a pang of sadness as he remembered rainy afternoons spent sheltering there with Rebecca when they were younger. Their weekly pocket money had always stretched to one

cinnamon bun between two and a steaming mug of hot chocolate each. That weekend ritual felt like a lifetime ago. Weekends were different now that Rebecca was at college. The seven-year age gap between them felt like a gulf.

Felix wandered over to the bakery and warmed his numb fingers in the hot air coming out of the vents in the kitchen wall. He scanned the menu in the  window as he rubbed his hands, despite not having any money. Inside, one of the customers, a middle-aged lady, had been sharing a slice of sponge cake with her little dog. The bell tinkled as she pushed the door open to leave.

Felix turned back towards the square and something strange caught his eye. A small man was standing on the wall that ran around the fountain. He definitely hadn't been there a few minutes ago.

He was hunched with his back to Felix, holding what looked like a long fishing rod. Next to him was a purple hat turned upside down. The man flicked something small and round from the end of his fishing rod into the hat.

Clink.

Felix stepped closer and edged around the circular fountain to get a better look. The hat was piled high with copper coins.

"Are those pennies from the fountain?" Felix asked in a more accusatory tone than he'd intended.

The fisherman flinched before turning towards Felix. His head was mostly covered by his hood, but Felix could just about pick out an elaborate moustache. Tufts of white hair poked out from under the hood, framing his face in a fog of cloud. The man's thick, white-flecked eyebrows were raised on his wrinkled forehead. Underneath, two startled eyes stared wide.

"Fe—" The man cut himself off. "You can see me?"

"Is that unusual?" Felix asked as he studied the man's appearance. He was dressed in a long overcoat and brown boots. There was something almost otherworldly about him.

"Yes," the man replied, still looking very startled.

"Oh," said Felix. "Well, I don't know why I wouldn't be able to see you when you're standing right up there on the fountain. It's pretty bold of you to do that in front of me. That's stealing, you know." He pointed at the small mountain of coins in the man's hat.

"I can see why you would say that." The man dipped the rod into the water and fished out another penny. *Clink*. "But I'm not doing anything wrong. Just collecting my wish wages. Here, I'll show you." He pulled a penny from his cap. "Look. What do you see there?"

Felix looked down at the wet, copper coin.

It looked like a normal penny to him. It had the familiar portcullis punched onto it.

"Turn it to the other side," the man said.

Felix turned the penny over. To his surprise, he saw a whiskered man's profile etched where the Queen's face should be. "It's *you*."

"Rupus Beewinkle," the man said, nodding in a friendly sort of way. "Nice to meet you. Do you see what the coin says?"

Felix peered at the tiny inscription written on the rim.

FELIX JONES. WISH 15973:

I wish my sister would like me again.

Felix inhaled sharply. Embarrassment at seeing his most personal wish revealed turned his cheeks pink. "But that's … that's impossible…"

"Oh, it's certainly not impossible. It would be a

bit on the tricky side to grant. But, in my experience, almost all wishes are *possible*." Rupus eyed Felix before adding, "This must all be quite a shock for you. I'll tell you what might help, a nice hot drink."

Rupus placed a few more pennies into Felix's hand. "Actually, I wouldn't mind one too. How about you get us a couple of the Blackbird Bakery's finest hot chocolates? Don't skimp on the marshmallows."

Felix looked down at his palm. "That's going to cost more than six pence."

"Oh, don't worry. I think you'll find you have enough." Rupus smiled knowingly as he ushered Felix towards the bakery door.

4

Whittlestone's Wishkeeper

Felix stepped into the bakery alone while Rupus waited outside. He took a deep breath as the door closed behind him.

"You're just in time. We're about to close! What can I get for you?" The woman behind the till smiled warmly. Regina Blackbird owned the bakery, but she was never too busy to serve a customer.

"Two hot chocolates, please," Felix said, eyeing the chalkboard menu with concern as he spoke. A hot chocolate cost two pounds fifteen pence.

Regina smiled and turned to scoop chocolate powder into some paper cups. As she did so, Felix

opened his clenched fist and, to his surprise, saw four gold pound coins along with a silver ten pence and a twenty pence piece.

"Wow," he said aloud.

"Everything OK?" Regina asked as she lifted a glass jar of marshmallows from a shelf and shook a few into each cup.

"Yes, everything's fine!" Felix handed her the money and thanked her, before he exited into the square.

Rupus Beewinkle was standing exactly where Felix had left him. He was now wearing his hat rather than his hood pulled up, and Felix noticed two very round ears poking out on either side of it.

"What are you? Some kind of magician?" Felix asked, trying not to stare at Rupus's long whiskery moustache.

"No, not a magician!" Rupus chuckled as if it was a ridiculous suggestion. "I'm a wishkeeper.

Whittlestone's wishkeeper, to be precise." He took one of the cups from Felix. "Ah, never enough marshmallows!" He sighed and plucked a few leaves from a nearby hedgerow.

Felix watched in amazement as Rupus dropped the green leaves into his cup. In an instant, each leaf had become a large, white marshmallow.

"Want one?" Rupus asked.

"No, thanks," Felix croaked.

"Suit yourself!" Rupus popped one into his mouth before chewing it with a smile of satisfaction.

"I've never heard of a wishkeeper," Felix said.

"No, of course you haven't. We wishkeepers are highly secretive creatures." Rupus puffed out his chest with pride.

"If you don't mind me asking, what is a wishkeeper exactly?"

"Finally! A useful question. What do you think a wishkeeper is?"

"Someone who grants wishes?" Felix said.

Rupus looked rather put out by this reply.

"Us wishkeepers do more than that," he said. "Try someone who listens to them. Risk-assesses them. *Grants* them. Monitors them. And most importantly *protects* them. Not that anyone ever thanks us for it. But still, a wishkeeper is a wishkeeper, and we do what we do." Rupus exhaled. "And we do it all in secret. We leave no trace of our existence. We're entirely invisible."

"Invisible?" Felix gave him a puzzled look. He could see Rupus clear as day.

"Usually," Rupus said.

"Are you telling me that no one else can see you?" Felix asked.

Rupus nodded.

"Well, how come I can?"

"I promise that I'm as surprised as you are. I didn't expect you to be able to see me either. But

I don't think it's any coincidence that you and I have met this afternoon."

Felix hesitated and then asked quietly, "Did you come here because of my wish?" He shuffled from foot to foot. He felt silly for having wished that, but he hadn't expected anyone else to find out about it. Who knew there was such a thing as a wishkeeper who granted wishes? Felix felt a spark of excitement run through him. Nothing magical had ever happened to him before.

Rupus continued to eat his marshmallows one by one as he spoke. "I received your wish just before I left the house. It was a very sad sort of wish. I wanted to come and check you were all right. While I was here I thought I might as well collect my pennies."

He ate another marshmallow and then lifted his eyes to the stars. "No," he said. "Perhaps there's more to it than that." His voice had taken on

a serious tone. "Maybe … perhaps … yes, I think this is *fate*."

He turned to meet Felix's eye. "I mean, here I am, all alone, watching Whittlestone's wishes fall to pieces. Who will help me? The Council of the Wishkeepers?" He raised an eyebrow. "No chance. But who else is there? *Nobody*. I'm an invisible creature. Not a soul in Whittlestone can see me. Not a soul can help me. Except *you*, that is!"

Rupus clapped Felix on the shoulder, keeping up the intense eye contact. It was making Felix a little uncomfortable. "It's *meant* to be. Finally, I have found my long-awaited apprentice. Here's to a long and happy partnership!" Rupus raised his paper cup in a toast.

Felix had no idea what was going on. Was he being offered a job? It certainly felt like he was. Should he say something? But what?

"Um, Mr Beewinkle..." he began. It was a very strange sort of name.

"Oh, don't be so formal! Please call me Rupus."

"OK, Rupus." Felix paused and took a gulp of hot chocolate to steady his nerves. "I've no idea what you're talking about. I mean – I'm not sure I believe in wishes—"

"Don't believe in wishes?" Rupus spluttered. "But you just made one." He paused before adding, "Although I do believe it's the first wish I've ever had from you. I'm sure I'd remember if..." His voice trailed off.

"This is *all* very unbelievable," Felix insisted.

"Of course." Rupus nodded. 'It's only natural, I suppose, to want more evidence. I'm afraid I can't grant your wish about your sister right away. It's a tricky one and goes against the guidelines... Not that I pay much attention to guidelines. Perhaps you could make a different wish? Just for demonstration

purposes. Any wish." He handed Felix a penny.

Felix stared at him. He didn't know what to ask for.

"Come on," Rupus urged. "There must be something else you want…"

Felix thought hard. "Well," he said. "There is something. Something that might help sort things out between me and Rebecca a bit. Or it might just save me having to walk home in the rain again. I wish—"

"Don't tell me, don't tell me!" Rupus said. "Wish it and throw the penny into the fountain."

Felix closed his eyes and did as Rupus had instructed. He waited. Nothing happened. He opened one eye and then the other. "Er…"

Rupus tutted. "Wishes don't appear out of thin air, Felix. They take work. Right, leave it with me and I'll see what I can do. It is wonderful to meet you, but I think we should part ways for now.

I've got half a dozen urgent wish snags to resolve this evening, including a particularly complex one involving an octopus. You can visit me tomorrow and we'll get started. I'll go over the wishkeeping paperwork and show you how it all works."

"Um, I'm not sure…"

"Oh, of course, you'll need the address!" Rupus beckoned for Felix to lower an ear to him. "One hundred and forty-three Silver Way," he whispered. "But that's a secret. Don't tell *anyone*. Can't take any risks these days."

"What do you mean?"

"Oh, I don't know. I just have a bad feeling… Things haven't felt right in Whittlestone recently… Better safe than sorry."

"One hundred and forty-three Silver Way," Felix repeated in a hushed voice. "I'll keep it a secret."

Rupus gave him a faint smile of gratitude and made to depart before turning back. "Oh, I'd better

give you this." He pulled what looked like an encyclopedia out of an impossibly small pocket and handed it to Felix.

Felix looked down at the cover.

A Complete Guide to Wishkeeping
Rules and Regulations

"You can read up on the basics before our lesson tomorrow. All the official stuff can be found in there, straight from The Council of the Wishkeepers." Rupus paused and then added, "You will come, won't you, Felix?" His voice wavered.

"Of course."

"You understand that it's very important. The future of Whittlestone depends on you helping me. And I do believe that fate has brought us together."

Felix nodded. He had no idea what Rupus was talking about, but the worry in the wishkeeper's eyes made him want to help. "I promise I'll come."

I wish for a bicycle, so that I won't have to ask Rebecca for any more lifts. (If it could be red too, that would be great.) Thanks.
Felix Jones, aged 10

5
A Complete Guide to Wishkeeping

Rebecca arrived home late for dinner that evening. Felix's mum raised an eyebrow as his sister sat down hastily at the table. "Nice of you to join us, Rebecca," she said dryly. "Have you remembered yet that you were supposed to pick your brother up from his football match? Really … it's not like we ask you to do much. Felix had to walk home in the rain."

"I didn't forget." Rebecca glared at Felix as if it was his fault she was in trouble. "He wasn't in the car park where I said I'd meet him."

"I *was* there," said Felix. "You must have been late."

"OK, so I was *five* minutes late. How was I supposed to know that you were going to storm off home?"

"You were definitely more than five minutes late," Felix murmured as he shovelled lasagne onto his plate. Once again, Rebecca was making him feel like a burden. But Felix's head was too full of thoughts of wishes and magic to care that much about his sister tonight. Had all that really happened to him? Was he really the only person in Whittlestone able to see Rupus Beewinkle?

It would have been nice to have someone to talk to about it all. At one point that would have been Rebecca, but she'd never believe him these days. Just a few years ago she would have been as excited about it all as he was.

Rebecca was still moaning about having to collect Felix. "He's ten! Can't he walk home by himself now? I had to."

"How was football?" Felix's dad interjected, putting the brakes on the brewing argument.

"Pretty awful," Felix replied. "As always." He didn't elaborate, even when his mum and dad both responded with looks of concern.

"What's the point in you going, then?" Rebecca asked coldly.

Felix didn't answer. He didn't feel like telling them all the truth: that since Max had moved away

he'd been on his own at school. He rarely had any after-school or weekend plans now. At least football gave him something to do.

"Where were you this afternoon, anyway?" Felix asked, in an attempt to change the subject.

"The cinema," Rebecca replied bluntly. Her new college finished early on Fridays.

"Thanks for the invite." Felix's voice was charged with sarcasm. He doubted he'd missed out on much. Rebecca was into horror films at the moment. The silly type where half the cast died in freak accidents and then turned into zombies at the end.

"You couldn't have come," she said. "It was rated a fifteen."

Felix bit his tongue. Recently, Rebecca had developed an annoying habit of constantly reminding him of his age. But he didn't want to be pulled into an argument. He was itching to get away and read more of the book Rupus had given him.

He'd barely managed a page or two before his dad had called him down for dinner.

As soon as he could, Felix dashed upstairs and closed his door behind him. The tidy bedroom felt like a cocoon of normality after his very strange day. It was a small room, but Felix's belongings were so well organized that it never felt claustrophobic. He straightened a stack of alphabetized comics and pulled Rupus's leather-backed book out from under his pillow. The book looked particularly out of place against the backdrop of his superhero bed sheets. Felix opened the dusty jacket and flicked through a few pages to find the section where he'd left off.

The Origin of Wishes

A wishkeeper may choose to grant a wish made via
any of the acceptable methods. These include, but
are not limited to, the following: wishing wells, penny
fountains, dandelions, stars, birthday candles and
wishbones. (For a complete list, see Appendix A.)
A wishkeeper must only accept wishes that originate
from their own district. Wishkeepers should keep
a record of each and every wish card they receive.
Records should include a note of the wish origin,
name and age of the wisher and an initial grade,
indicating suitability for fulfilment.

If a wish card from another district has been delivered in error,
please inform the Council immediately, so that it can
reinforce the existing wish boundaries.

Wish Grades

Grade One: A Highly Suitable Wish

The wish is realistic and appears well thought through. Granting the wish will require only minimal magic, and there are no foreseeable maintenance issues. Grade One Wishes should be granted as a priority.

Grade Two: Requires Further Assessment

The wish is somewhat far-fetched but possible. Granting the wish will require considerable magic and complications are possible (if not likely). A risk assessment should be carried out at the wishkeeper's leisure, but Grade Two Wishes should not be prioritized.

Grade Three: Pie in the Sky

A naive or unrealistic wish with the potential for serious complications. These wishes must be noted for record keeping but should not be granted, unless a permit has been issued by The Council of the Wishkeepers. Guidance on how to apply for a Grade Three Permit can be found on page 107. (Please note: this is a lengthy process with a five- to seven-month wait time.)

Grade Four: Ungrantable Wishes

A wish that falls outside of official wishkeeping regulations. Common examples include a wish that involves the extension of life (or, indeed, the creation of life); a wish that involves altering a person's core feelings (e.g. love charms); a malicious wish; or a wish of significant magnitude (i.e. one that would change the course of national/ global history). These wishes cannot under any circumstance be granted, since the repercussions would be entirely unmanageable for even the most experienced wishkeeper.

6
The Wolf of Nightmares

Felix stayed up reading late into the evening. It was almost midnight by the time he stowed the book safely under his bed and crawled under his duvet. Magical terminology jingled around in his head as he lowered it onto his pillow.

At first, Felix felt certain he wouldn't be able to sleep. He was far too excited about the events of the day. But it wasn't long until his eyes closed, and the recurring nightmare swept into his mind like a black storm cloud.

The dream began in the usual way. Felix was surrounded by complete darkness. Then, out of the shadows, a wolf-man emerged. "Why are you still here, Felix?" it growled. "Nobody wants you."

The words hit Felix like a knife in the chest. "They do," he whispered.

"Who wants you?" the wolf-man asked.

There was a long pause as Felix searched for an answer. "My family," he croaked finally.

The creature let out a bark of laughter. "Rebecca doesn't want you here. Why don't you just disappear, Felix? No one will notice you're gone."

"They will," Felix managed to reply. But the wolf-man's words were sharp in his heart.

"You're useless, Felix. Nobody needs you. Nobody will miss you."

Felix had no reply to this. He squeezed his eyes shut so as not to see the creature's victorious grin. Suddenly, a thought bolted into Felix's mind. He did have an answer.

"Rupus," Felix said. "Rupus Beewinkle needs me."

The creature's red eyes flashed with fury.

"What did you just say?"

"RUPUS BEEWINKLE NEEDS ME!"

Felix was woken abruptly by a noise on the landing. He reached for his bedside lamp and switched it on, immediately feeling safer in the warm glow of the light.

Creak.

Felix sat bolt upright and listened as soft footsteps made their way down the corridor. Then he crept to the door and peered out.

"What are you doing up?" Rebecca asked as she eyed him through the crack in the doorway.

Felix swung his bedroom door open and shrugged. "Nightmare." His heart was still thudding inside his chest, but he didn't want to make a fuss in front of Rebecca.

"The one with the wolf-man again?" Rebecca yawned. "You're such a baby, Felix."

Felix didn't say a word. He was still furious that his mum had told Rebecca about his nightmares. The horrible recurring dreams had been going on

for weeks now. But it was just another excuse for Rebecca to treat him like a baby.

"Did you just get home?" Felix said, changing the subject. He hadn't heard her go out again after dinner, but she was dressed in dark jeans and a black leather jacket. "What time is it?"

"One a.m. But it's Friday night and *I* have a social life."

"I have a social life too."

They both knew this was a lie. "So, do you have plans for tomorrow?" she asked.

Felix paused. He couldn't mention Rupus. "Why do you care?" he asked, mildly hopeful that Rebecca wanted to hang out for once.

"I don't. I just want to make sure you aren't going to mope around here on your own all day."

"Oh. Did you want to—"

"I've got film club," Rebecca said quickly.

"Fine," Felix said, trying not to feel hurt.

It wasn't so long ago that he and Rebecca had spent every Saturday morning together watching box sets of cartoons, but now she had more important things to do, like film club and her new part-time job. And she spent her evenings out late with other college students. "I'm going to a friend's house anyway," he told her.

Rebecca raised an eyebrow as if she knew it wasn't true. "Glad to hear it. Night, then."

"Good night," Felix said as he closed his door, feeling a pang of loneliness.

7
A Wish Granted

After a night of restless dreams, Felix woke and pulled back his curtains. In the far distance, a tiny patch of glistening sea was just about visible. Felix glanced down at the front garden below and blinked in disbelief. The bicycle he'd wished for was parked on the driveway. It was exactly as he'd imagined it.

Felix burst out of the front door, still barefoot and in his pyjamas. The shiny red bicycle was a thing of beauty. He inched closer, wincing as he walked on the gravel, and inspected the metallic red paintwork. It didn't have a single scratch.

Every detail was immaculate, right down to the black leather seat, which had been stitched with tiny gold stars.

There was a note around its handlebars:

Do you believe in wishes now?

Felix smiled from ear to ear. A glistening silver bell sat on top of one of the handlebars and he reached out and dinged it. His heart soared. He'd never owned anything this beautiful. He couldn't wait to try it out.

"Wow. Where did that come from?"

Felix turned to see Rebecca standing in the open front doorway. She looked impressed.

"Er … a friend," Felix replied.

"I thought you didn't have any friends. It's *nice*," she added begrudgingly. "So, what's the deal? This friend is lending it to you, or what?"

"I guess so."

"Does this mean I won't have to give you any more lifts home from school?"

Felix nodded. "You're up early. Heading to film club?" he asked, noticing Rebecca was carrying a film script and her car keys.

"Yeah, I'm supposed to be there already. But Mum's asked me to pick up bread first, so I'm going to be really late now."

"I can get the bread." Felix nodded towards his bike. "The Blackbird Bakery is only, what, a ten-minute cycle ride away?"

"Oh," said Rebecca. "That would be amazing." She handed him a five-pound note.

"No problem at all," Felix replied. It was nice to feel useful for once.

"I'll get going, then." Rebecca opened the car door before turning back to say, "Sorry I was late yesterday."

Felix couldn't believe his ears. An apology from Rebecca was like rain in a desert.

"I promise I didn't completely forget you. I just got distracted with friends."

Felix nodded, too surprised to speak.

"Enjoy your new bike!" Rebecca gave him a wave as she got into the car.

"Thanks," Felix called after her.

And Rebecca turned and smiled at him for the first time in months.

Felix dashed back upstairs and pulled on some clothes and shoes. Within a couple of minutes, he was back outside, fastening the strap on the brand-new helmet. He wheeled the bike onto the empty road and leaped on.

The wheels let out a soft whispering noise as they turned, like they were telling him a secret. *Wisha. Wisha. Wisha.* He leaned into the handlebars and the bicycle carried him down the slope of the street.

The boy and the bicycle moved as one, soaring towards town. This was his ticket to independence. No more asking for lifts from Rebecca. No more feeling like a burden. Maybe now Rebecca would stop treating him like such a baby.

8
143 Silver Way

After a successful trip to the bakery, Felix cycled to Silver Way. He leaned into the slight dip of the road as he rounded the corner, and began to scan the numbers on the doors. He couldn't see number 143, but he knew Rupus Beewinkle's house must be here somewhere.

Ahead of him, a railway bridge arched over the end of the street. Felix stopped by it and got off his bike. Then he walked back on himself. The last house number read 141. Rupus's house was nowhere to be seen.

Stumped, Felix walked along the pavement and

under the bridge, just to check there were no more houses beyond.

And there, under the railway bridge, Felix noticed a small doorway in the brickwork. Three brass numbers were hanging on the door's peeling paintwork: 143.

Felix steadied himself and knocked on the little door. He waited so long for an answer that he knocked again.

Eventually, the door creaked open and Rupus's whiskered face peered out. He was wearing what looked like an old-fashioned nightcap and his eyes were as wide as teacups.

"Felix!" he exclaimed. "I wasn't expecting you so early." Rupus looked exhausted.

"But it's ten a.m."

"Is it? I was sleeping. Something terrible happened with one of my wishes last night and I didn't get a wink of sleep until after dawn."

"Oh. Maybe I should come back another day, then?" Felix offered, feeling a bit disappointed.

"Tomorrow?" Rupus suggested.

"I'm seeing my grandparents tomorrow."

"The next day, then?"

"I have school on Monday."

"School?" Rupus looked puzzled, as if he was trying to recall what school was. "Remind me, Felix, is school absolutely obligatory?"

Felix nodded slowly.

"Right, then. I suppose we'll just have to work around it. How often do you go to school?"

"Every day?" Felix replied, wondering how on

earth Rupus didn't know this already. "Except for Saturdays and Sundays."

"You're telling me you can only work on Saturdays and Sundays?" Rupus looked crestfallen.

"Yes. So, if you need to go back to sleep now, I can just come next Saturday. It's no trouble." Felix was itching to learn more about the magic of wishkeeping, but there was no real reason to rush. At least he had the book to read while he waited.

Rupus shook his head. "No. Certainly not! There is far too much to do. Your wishkeeping lessons cannot possibly wait another week. The wishes of Whittlestone are falling to pieces as we speak. We'll start right now, as a matter of urgency."

Rupus rubbed the sleep from his eyes and stepped backwards into the very messy hallway to allow Felix inside.

Felix paused. Was he really going to do this? Was he going to be Rupus's apprentice? He took one more look at Rupus's worried expression and ducked through the little doorframe into the house. The proportions of the front door, the hallway and everything in it were much smaller than usual. But Felix found he could just about stand comfortably once inside.

"Come through and find a seat." Rupus looked him up and down. "My, my, I never thought I'd see the day. My apprentice is here at last."

Felix made his way into the cramped living room, feeling very unsure about what exactly would be expected of him. He looked around for somewhere to sit. Almost every surface was littered with papers, and there were empty teacups dotted around the room. In the end, he perched on a footstool while Rupus settled into his desk chair.

"Isn't it a bit gloomy working in here?" Felix was starting to feel a bit sorry for Rupus, living all alone in this dark, cluttered house under a railway bridge.

There wasn't the slightest hint of natural daylight, since there were no windows at all.

"Gloomy? No, no," Rupus said. "There's no gloom in Snugwarm."

"Snugwarm?"

"Ah, yes, it's my pet name for the house. Snugwarm." Rupus looked around the room with an affectionate gaze. "A hidden house. Completely safe. No one can find Snugwarm, unless they've been given the address."

Felix nodded slowly. He'd never heard of anyone having a pet name for their house. Couples, children and best friends had nicknames but not houses.

He watched as Rupus busied himself, turning on lights. First, he flicked the switch for a chandelier in the centre of the ceiling, then two floor lamps, three table lamps, an angle-poise light on the desk and finally a long string of fairy lights adorning the fireplace.

"There. Lovely, isn't it?" Rupus smiled a satisfied smile and sat back in the desk chair.

The lights were cosy, but Felix was struggling to see past the clutter. "Have you always lived here?"

"All of my adult life. Whittlestone was my first posting as a newly qualified wishkeeper and I've never left. Some wishkeepers enjoy a change of scene now and then, but I have always felt Snugwarm is home."

"So, there are more of you, then? Wishkeepers, I mean."

"Yes, one wishkeeper household per district," Rupus explained, and Felix remembered reading something about that in the wishkeepers' guide. "Each wishkeeper is responsible for keeping on top of all the wishes within their particular village or town. It's quite a solitary job if you don't have a family, but an extremely important one."

Felix nodded and Rupus went on, "I'm sure

you'll have noticed that until recently Whittlestone has been a particularly hopeful sort of place?"

"I guess it's fairly upbeat here." Felix shrugged. "My mum says it's the sea air."

"*Fairly* upbeat, you say?" Rupus tapped a pencil absent-mindedly. "Would it surprise you to learn that Whittlestone was the most wishful place in the entire country until a month ago? More wishes per kilometre than any other district."

"Really? Well, congratulations. That's quite an achievement."

"*Congratulations?* Commiserations would be more appropriate. Do you have any idea how much work it is trying to keep up with all those wishes?"

Rupus waved a hand at a huge stack of paper. "Those are last month's wish cards. I only managed to grant a handful. Too busy trying to fix all of the wishes that have been going wrong."

Felix leaned forward and picked up one wish card at random.

> I wish I could grow a butternut squash big enough to win this year's harvest festival prize.
>
> Roger Jelly, aged 52

"Oh, so these are the wishes?" Felix asked, leafing through a few of the other cards. It felt nosy, like reading someone else's diary. "What are the little symbols at the top?"

"That's the origin stamp. They signify the origin of the wish. For example, if it's a penny-fountain wish, then the note will have a circle at the top, and those always arrive via my toaster." Rupus shrugged. "There's no real logic to it. Wishes on stars drop through my skylight, so I suppose that makes a kind of sense. Awfully disruptive to sleep, though,

you know." Rupus's eyes seemed suddenly dark with tiredness. "I'm forever finding wishbone wishes crumpled at the bottom of my teacup – those are the soggy ones." He waved at a row of cards drying on top of the radiator.

"And this one?" Felix pushed Roger Jelly's card under Rupus's nose.

"Ah, yes, a dandelion wish. Those are quite rare. They arrive directly into my hat." He lifted the purple woollen hat from his head to reveal another neatly folded card inside. "Ah ha. Another one." Rupus threw the card on top of the pile.

"I can see you've had a lot to keep up with," Felix said. "Do you have to grant them all? Aren't there any" – Felix remembered what he'd read last night – "ungrantable wishes?"

"Oh … well … some… There's no obligation for a wishkeeper to grant every single one. But these are *treasured* wishes. They tug on the heartstrings.

I can't help but want to grant most of them."

"I see." Felix paused. "I'm sure it won't be the end of the world if you don't have time to grant Roger Jelly's wish about the butternut squash."

"Yes. Well, that one is ruled out anyway. I've already granted somebody else's wish to win the harvest festival. I planted a whopper pumpkin in Mr Green's garden last week, so the first prize is his. Anyway, it's not just the backlog of wish notifications that I can't keep up with." Rupus sighed. "It's the all the wish snagging. I've had dozens of wish snags this past week, including the particularly awful one that kept me up last night." Rupus looked like he was on the verge of tears. "I'm just so glad you are here, Felix."

"Listen, Mr Beewinkle – I mean, Rupus – I need to tell you something." Felix tried to gather his thoughts. "I'm not sure I'm the right person to be your apprentice. It sounds like you have some very important work and, well, I'm not…" Felix was struggling to string a sentence together. "I'm not very good at most things," he concluded.

"Nonsense, boy. You don't even know what I'm asking you to do yet. How could you possibly know whether or not you are capable of doing it?"

Felix thought back to yesterday's own goal on the football pitch. That was fairly typical of Felix's contribution to most activities. Maybe it was because he was a younger sibling, but Felix had spent most of his life feeling like a burden. He shrugged. "Just a gut feeling, I suppose."

"Oh, Felix. I need you." Rupus looked as if the weight of the world was stacked on his frail shoulders. "Anyway, it's your moral duty to take on this apprenticeship. The very existence of Whittlestone as we know it depends on our work. I will not let the wishes of the people of Whittlestone be torn apart. Not on my watch." He puffed his

chest out a little
and the buttons
on his nightshirt
pulled tight. "Are
you with me?"

Felix thought about
it for a moment or two.
He doubted he'd be
any use, but Rupus
really seemed to
need his help.
"Probably, yes,"
he said.

"*Probably?*" Rupus slammed a book onto the desk before standing up and marching into the hallway.

Felix followed him to the front door and watched as he pulled on a pair of thick leather boots. With a great huff, Rupus threw a coat on

over the top of his pyjamas. "We're going out," he announced. "There's no point in training you until you understand the importance of our work."

"Where are we going?" Felix asked.

"I'm going to show you what it looks like when a wish goes wrong. You need to see what kept me awake last night."

9

A Bicycle Built for Two

Felix followed Rupus out of the front door and into the tunnel beyond. Rupus headed straight for Felix's bicycle. "With just a few tweaks, this should easily carry the two of us," he said.

Rupus reached into his breast pocket and removed a small leather case the size of a pocket notebook. Half a dozen metal instruments were lined up inside it. Rupus selected a small golden blade, with which he carefully cut along the seam of the bicycle seat.

Felix watched in dismay. "What…? What are you doing?"

Rupus looked at him in surprise. "We can't both ride on one seat, can we?"

Felix winced as Rupus used a chisel and hammer to break the seat in half. "Will you be able to fix it again?" he asked. It didn't feel fair for Rupus to be making modifications to his bicycle without even asking him.

"Of course! I made this entire bicycle out of three umbrellas and a coat stand, if you can believe it. Now ... where did I put the..." Rupus began rooting around in his pocket. "Ah ha. Here it is." He opened a small vial of silver powder and sprinkled it over both halves of the seat. *"Atchoo!"* he sneezed. "Try not to breathe it in. This is instant fixing powder. I don't have time to create a new seat from scratch, but I'm hoping this will do the trick. Don't look so worried, Felix. I'll put the bike back the way it was."

As Rupus was speaking, the two halves of the bicycle seat suddenly branched out from one

another and grew into separate cushioned seats. Rupus nodded with satisfaction. Then he reached down and gripped one of the pedals with a pair of tongs. He pulled the pedals upwards by ten centimetres and then put his tools away. "On you get, then, Felix." He gestured towards the back seat.

"Are you driving?" Felix asked. He was feeling rather shaken up by what had just happened to his beloved bike.

"Well, I'm the one who knows where we're going. Hop on quickly. We don't have any time to spare."

Felix clambered onto the back seat before helping Rupus to climb onto the front one. The wishkeeper's feet didn't reach anywhere near the ground, but they slotted into the newly adjusted pedals perfectly. In an instant, they were off.

"Is there any need to go so fast?" Felix shouted, clinging onto the back of Rupus's coat, as Rupus swerved into a side street heading out of town.

"Yes," Rupus replied simply. "Mind if I sing?"

"What?" This journey was getting stranger by the minute. "Why would you sing?"

"Passes the time. Keeps my spirits up. And prevents sweat."

"Sure." Felix attempted to shrug as much as anyone can shrug while they are clinging on for dear life. Rupus was easily the most unpredictable person Felix had ever met. But something told him he could trust his strange new friend.

"Oh, Whittlestone, how does thou fair?"
Rupus belted out the lyrics twice as loudly as Felix had anticipated:

"Do not fear, your wishkeeper is near.
Oh, Whittlestone, how does thou fair?
How does thou fair this bright day?"

The volume of Rupus's singing was just as surprising as his cycling speed. By the time they reached their destination, Felix's stomach was in his throat and his ears were ringing from Rupus's bellowing song.

"Here we are," Rupus cried as he suddenly slammed on the brakes.

Both of them lurched forward off the bike and tumbled onto a grassy bank.

"Is that the Half Moon Theatre?" Felix asked, looking up at the blackened shell of a building. He'd visited it plenty of times for Christmas pantomimes and school trips and had always thought of it as a magical place. The building was barely recognizable, and there was no trace left of its jolly yellow façade.

"It *was* the Half Moon Theatre," Rupus corrected him. "Now it's mainly charcoal."

Felix stared at the once splendid building. The billboard outside, usually awash with colourful posters, was covered in a thick layer of soot.

"I got the wish snag notification yesterday evening, just after dark," Rupus added.

"Wish snag?" Felix asked. Rupus had an annoying habit of talking as if Felix should somehow understand everything he was saying.

"Wish snag *notification*. A message to let me know that something has gone wrong with one of

80

my wishes. Usually, it's just small things, like little teething issues. But this was the worst wish snag I've ever had. The entire building was on fire. I got myself a nasty burn trying to put it out." He winced as he rolled up one sleeve of his coat to reveal a bandage.

"You should never ever go into a burning building. Everyone knows that," Felix pointed out, feeling both impressed by Rupus's bravery and concerned about his safety assessments.

"Oh, a little burn is the least of my worries now. I have spent thirty-six years working on this place. It was Tom Chillwell's childhood wish. Do you know how hard it is to keep a theatre up and running in a sleepy seaside town? I wasn't going to stand back and let a fire destroy all that work. But it's more than just this wish snag. Something isn't right in Whittlestone. In fact, something is very, very wrong."

Rupus took a deep breath. "A bit of wish

snagging here or there is normal, especially seeing as I grant a lot of big wishes. It's natural for those to go off-track sometimes. But over the last couple of months, I've been seeing *endless* wish snagging. The wish snags are off the scale, Felix. I think there's only one explanation…" A dark expression fell over Rupus's face. "Something or *someone* is deliberately attacking my wishes."

"But who would want to do that?" Felix asked.

"I have my suspicions."

There was a noise near the theatre and they both turned to see two fire officials emerge from the building accompanied by a crestfallen-looking man.

"That's Tom Chillwell," Rupus said with a sigh. "He's dreamed of running a theatre since he was nine years old. That's thirty-six years of him wishing and me working hard to make it happen. Then, in a matter of minutes, a fire appears out of nowhere and it's all gone in the blink of an eye."

Rupus gave another long sigh. "Stay here and try to look inconspicuous. I just need to pop inside for a minute and fix a few of the load-bearing walls. Tom's insurance will cover most of the damage but only if the building can be salvaged." Rupus set off towards the tumbledown ruin.

"Be careful," Felix called after him. He felt a sudden sense of doom fall over him like a heavy curtain. He froze, rooted to the spot. His neck prickled, and he checked over his shoulder, but no one was there.

A few minutes later Rupus re-emerged from the building with sooty cheeks.

"Done!" he said briskly. He seemed a little chirpier than before. "Should be enough to save the building. It'll be months before it's fully restored, but Tom will get there in the end. He's the perseverant sort." Rupus looked at Felix with furrowed brows. "Do you see why I brought you

here? I needed you to see this. I needed you to see how terrible it is when wishes go wrong."

"Yes, well, I see that now. Can we head back home?" Felix asked, anxious to leave. "I feel really on edge being here."

A flicker of fear crossed Rupus's face. "Can you describe how you feel?"

"Like I say, on edge." Felix didn't really know how else to explain the strange emotion that was now knotted deep in his stomach. It was worse than any nightmare.

"Do you feel like we're all doomed?" Rupus asked, looking very serious.

Felix nodded slowly. That was exactly how he felt.

"That confirms it, then." Rupus's eyes were wide with despair. "My worst fear. I knew it! There is a *wishsnatcher* in Whittlestone."

10
THE WISHSNATCHER
OF WHITTLESTONE

"Come quickly," Rupus told Felix, as he took him down a side alley that led to the back of the theatre. At the end of the alley was a hedgerow that marked the boundary between the theatre and an overgrown field beyond. Felix reluctantly made his way towards it. The sense of dread filled him from head to toe. He had no idea what a wishsnatcher was, but he didn't want to bump into one any time soon.

"Do you feel better or worse now?" Rupus asked solemnly.

"Much worse. I feel worse than I've ever felt in all my life."

"Yes, I sense that too. A wishsnatcher is the only creature I know of that can fill a place with this much misery. A creature of pure despair. They leave a trail of gloom wherever they go."

Felix looked about himself nervously. "Maybe we should head back to Snugwarm," he suggested. He couldn't bear to stay here any longer. The sense of hopelessness was overwhelming.

"Soon. But we need to work out where the wishsnatcher's lair is first," Rupus told him. "We're safe for now. Wishsnatchers only venture out at night. They live solitary lives, hidden in dark places. I'm sure this one is living somewhere near by."

Felix and Rupus both looked into the distance, across the expanse of empty fields that lay beyond Whittlestone. A huge industrial building loomed on the horizon. Felix recognized it as the old

abandoned colliery. Coal mining had been a major industry for Whittlestone back in the day.

"Dark places like coal mines?" Felix asked. He shuddered. The abandoned colliery had always given him the creeps.

"Exactly." Rupus nodded sombrely. He stared hard at the coal mines. "A wishsnatcher's den in Whittlestone would explain everything. That's why I wake up to dozens of new wish snags every morning. The wishsnatcher is attacking my wishes at night."

"Why do they attack wishes?" Felix asked, feeling alarmed at the thought of a monster roaming the streets of Whittlestone while everyone slept.

"Wishsnatchers feed off despair," Rupus explained. "They hate wishes and wishkeepers. Given the chance, a wishsnatcher would capture a wishkeeper. I should thank my lucky stars that I got away with nothing more than a burn last night."

"What would happen if—" Felix stopped halfway through the question, unsure how to finish it.

"If the wishsnatcher caught me?" Rupus finished the question for him. "Every wish in Whittlestone would be destroyed."

"*Every* wish?" Felix's voice was a whisper.

"The wishsnatcher would pluck the wishes from my soul, one by one." Rupus's voice was shaking. "Eventually every wish I've ever granted would be obliterated, and so would I."

"Obliterated?" Felix repeated. It seemed like an extreme sort of word.

"Yes," said Rupus. "A wish cannot survive without the wishkeeper who granted it and a wishkeeper cannot survive without their wishes. If the wishsnatcher gets his hands on me, that's the end of all my wishes. And the end of me!"

Rupus was wringing his hands as he spoke. "I wouldn't be surprised if last night's fire was a deliberate attempt to draw me out of my hidden house." He inhaled sharply. "If so, then I was just a whisker away from utter destruction." His eyes filled with emotion as he stared despairingly at the coal mines.

"It's OK, Rupus." Felix tried his best to reassure him, even though he felt like sinking into a pit of gloom too. "You got away. And now that you know about the wishsnatcher, you can do something about it, right?"

Rupus nodded and looked a little more hopeful. "Yes, yes, of course. All is not lost. Something must have fended the creature off last night."

"What sort of thing would have done that?"

"Oh, anything good," Rupus replied vaguely. "Anything hopeful, anything brave, anything optimistic. Wishsnatchers can't bear to be around those kinds of feelings. Perhaps the bravery of a fire fighter, or the hopeful thoughts of the neighbours

looking on… There was quite a crowd by the time I got here. Those small things are very powerful, you know, Felix. They can tip the balance. A wishsnatcher cannot be in the presence of true hope. That's why they hate wishes so much."

"I see. Maybe Whittlestone will be OK, then? So long as people remain hopeful?"

"Remaining hopeful is no easy thing. Not when wishes are snagging left right and centre." Rupus frowned. "We have an enormous task ahead of us. We must keep Whittlestone afloat. So long as there is hope, the creature cannot win. We must not let Whittlestone fall into the hands of the wishsnatcher."

11

ThE WishsnatchER ExtinguishER

There was no singing on the journey home. Felix took his turn on the pedals, cycling with a weary heart. Rupus didn't say a word until Felix stopped the bike under the bridge by his hidden front door.

As they clambered off the bicycle, it morphed back into a single-seater. Just a few hours ago Felix's biggest concern had been Rupus's alterations to his prized bicycle. It seemed such a little thing now that he had a wishsnatcher to worry about,

although he was glad to see his
bike back to its beautiful self.

Felix followed Rupus, who had
rushed straight inside the house and
scrambled to the understairs cupboard.
Felix stood in the narrow hallway and watched
Rupus rifle through a mountain of dusty junk. He
pulled out a few suitcases, then an assortment of
feather dusters and finally a vacuum cleaner. With a
great puff, Rupus clambered over the
vacuum cleaner and disappeared
behind a variety of coats.

"Aha," came a muffled
voice, followed by a faint
grunting noise.

Then, "Thank goodness," and another grunt. Felix got the impression that Rupus was lifting something heavy.

Moments later, Rupus emerged from the cupboard. He was pink-cheeked and cradling a red metal cylindrical tank. It was covered in a thick layer of dust and bore many similarities to a fire extinguisher.

"What on *earth* is that?" Felix asked.

Rupus wiped away a small patch of dust.

"This is our only weapon against the wishsnatcher," he said as he heaved the metal tank through the hallway and set it down by the front door. "At least we're ready for an attack now."

Felix eyed the device

sceptically. It didn't look particularly powerful. "What exactly is a vanquisher?" he asked.

"It's a defensive weapon, capable of destroying a wishsnatcher in seconds. Right, no time to waste. We need to make a plan." Rupus gestured for Felix to go into the front room.

Felix sat back down on the same footstool he had earlier and waited while Rupus fetched something from the kitchen. He could hear cupboard doors being opened and closed. He eyed the clock on the cluttered mantelpiece. It was late afternoon. He didn't really understand why Rupus was prioritizing food during a wishkeeping emergency.

Rupus returned with two generous portions of apple cake and a couple of mugs. "Cake and snorlicks is the only way to get us through a conversation on wishsnatchers. Eat up!"

Felix had never heard of snorlicks before. It was

wonderfully creamy, like a hot chocolate, except it was white and quite custardy. From the first sip, it filled him with a sense of calm.

"Wishsnatchers are not the merriest subject for an apprentice's first day. But it's vital that you understand what we are up against." Rupus swallowed a mouthful of cake and then cleared his throat. "Centuries ago, wishsnatchers roamed the British Isles freely, spreading despair wherever they went. When I was young, every wishkeeper household had a vanquisher by the front door, just in case a wishsnatcher should strike. My mother used to sleep with our vanquisher under her pillow.

"Fortunately, we didn't ever have to use one, because the wishkeepers fought back and over time wishsnatcher numbers decreased. Fifty years ago, The Council of the Wishkeepers claimed to have destroyed the last and final wishsnatcher."

Rupus's eyes glazed over with a far-off look.

"But us wishkeepers have relaxed too much. And now… Well, I have no doubt that a wishsnatcher is closing in on Whittlestone. Just look at the wishfulness gauge."

Rupus gestured at what looked like a mahogany grandfather clock in the corner of the room. Instead of a clock face, it had a scale of numbers.

The golden arrow on the dial was hovering between one and two.

"Before this week, I haven't had a wishfulness reading below a three point five for over thirty years," Rupus said. "Now look at it! The arrow drops lower every single day. If wishfulness disappears from the air entirely, then nobody will be able to make any new wishes. And then it's just a matter of time before Whittlestone falls into utter despair." Tears glistened in the wishkeeper's eyes. He sat back down in his chair and let out a puff of exasperation. "It's all my fault."

"It's not your fault a wishsnatcher is attacking Whittlestone," Felix said, feeling sorry for Rupus.

"But it *is* my fault. Do you remember what I was saying about Whittlestone being the most wishful place in the country? That's why the wretched creature has come here. It's *my* fault that this is happening. I've granted too many wishes. I've made Whittlestone irresistible! Thanks to me, Whittlestone has thousands of wishes to attack and

thousands of hearts to fill with despair."

Rupus buried his head in his hands. "I've tempted the last wishsnatcher out of its den and now it's growing stronger every day." Rupus reached for a lace doily and dabbed at the tears gathering in his wrinkled eyes. "I'm so sorry, Felix."

"It's OK." Felix pulled a crumpled tissue from his pocket. He smoothed it out before handing it to Rupus. "We'll find a way to fix things. You're not on your own any more. I'll try my very best to help." Felix glanced at the clock. He really needed to get home for dinner soon, but he didn't want to leave Rupus in such a state.

"Thank you. That makes me feel a lot better. I'll notify The Council of the Wishkeepers about the wishsnatcher. But knowing them, they'll take for ever to do anything about it. In the meantime, we've got to keep Whittlestone afloat. We can't let the wishfulness gauge drop any lower. We can't let the

wishsnatcher gain any more ground."

"What do you need from me?" Felix asked.

"I need you to help me get on top of the wish snags. We need to repair some of the damage. The wish snags arrive here." Rupus shuffled towards the wishfulness gauge and opened a door in the chest of the device. He tore a section off the scroll inside and handed it to Felix. The text was small and hard to read.

WISH 15732
Condition: CRITICAL
Immediate action required
Detail: factory malfunction

WISH 1965
Condition: seriously threatened
Urgent wish maintenance required
Detail: Fluffy has been missing since 7 a.m. on Tuesday

WISH 2793
Condition: deteriorating
Wishkeeping required
Detail: bakery profits down 80% year on year

"The snags won't make proper sense until you match them with the original wishes," Rupus explained. "I keep a record of each wish in the files over there. They should be in order … mainly."

Felix eyed the wishkeeping files stacked precariously on the shelf above Rupus's desk. They were brimming with loose papers. They looked like they needed sorting out. Maybe alphabetizing would work.

"That sounds like paperwork. I can do that." Felix scanned the snowstorm of papers littering the room. Organizing was just about the only thing he was good at. But he was *very* good at it.

"Really?" Rupus looked doubtful. "It's all such a mess."

"I'm the library assistant at school. I can help you file all of this in no time." It felt good to be useful for once. Maybe Rupus was right? Maybe fate really had brought them together. "I should get

101

home now, before it's dark. But I'll come back as soon as I can tomorrow," Felix assured him.

"I thought you said you couldn't come tomorrow?"

"I'm supposed to see my grandparents, but I'll make an excuse."

Rupus nodded appreciatively. "Until tomorrow, then," he said as he showed Felix to the door.

Felix exited into the shadow of the tunnel. He turned briefly to wave goodbye. Rupus gave him a brave smile and a salute before closing the door.

12
Rupus Beewinkle's Most Illegal Wish

Felix arrived at Snugwarm feeling motivated. He was keen to make as much progress as possible while his family was out visiting his grandparents for a few hours. He'd complained of a sore stomach to his mum, and for once she hadn't asked many questions. When he knocked on the door of 143 Silver Way, Rupus was still in his dressing gown. He was in a morose mood.

"I had twenty-three wish snag notifications last night," Rupus told him.

"Well, we'd better get going, then," Felix replied,

heading into the front room. He tried to sound as positive as he could. There didn't seem any point sinking into despair. "Where shall we start? Maybe I can sort the wish snags into chronological order?"

"Yes, yes," said Rupus, distracted with worry. "And I'll send a message to The Council of the Wishkeepers about the wishsnatcher. I'm sure they won't believe me. They'll probably think I'm going potty. I've always gotten the impression that they see me as a bit of a loose cannon." He raised his hands in a gesture of dismay.

As Rupus busied himself with the wishofax messaging machine, Felix cast an eye around the room, feeling a bit overwhelmed already. It reminded him of the one time, years ago, when he'd offered to help Rebecca tidy her bedroom.

Rupus's records were in chaos. Just getting the wish snags into priority order took the whole morning. Rupus was largely useless. He kept walking around the room, tugging his whiskers and just moving things from one pile to another. All the while, he had one eye on his wishofax machine, waiting for a reply.

"Why don't you go and make us snorlicks?" Felix suggested in an attempt to gain some peace and quiet.

Mercifully, Rupus agreed, before deciding to get washed and dressed and prepare an early lunch. It gave Felix some time to concentrate.

Once he had ordered the wish snags,

he began the task of looking up the original wishes in the wish files.

There were ten large wish files on the shelf above the desk. Felix was surprised to see that Rupus had, in fact, managed to keep the files in some sort of order. Somewhat frustratingly, volume VII was missing.

Felix rifled through the desk drawers, checked in cupboards and eventually found the missing volume lying open under the sofa. It was as if Rupus had been deliberately hiding it. Felix sighed and lifted it onto the desk. Immediately, one of the entries on the open page caught his eye. It was from ten years ago.

I wish I had a little brother or sister.
Rebecca Jones, aged 6
Penny fountain wish
Grade 4

Felix's heart froze at the sight of his sister's name.

Just at that moment, Rupus came bustling back into the room with a trayful of lunch. The elderly wishkeeper took one look at what Felix was reading and dropped the tray. He turned sheet-white.

"Rupus?" Felix said nervously. "What is this?"

Rupus refused to meet his eye. "I'm so sorry, Felix. You weren't meant to see that... I should have told you."

"Did you – did you grant this?" Felix's voice was shaking. "Did you grant Rebecca's wish?"

"Yes," Rupus murmured with his eyes lowered.

Felix stared back down at the wish entry. Suddenly he felt dizzy and the words seemed to swim around on the page.

"The baby was born nine months later," Rupus told him. "Just in time for Christmas."

"Are you – are you telling me…" Felix began. "I was born on the twenty-third of December ten years ago." His heart sank like a stone. "No. You couldn't have. It's against all the rules."

"I know." Rupus shook his head, still avoiding eye contact. "I'm so sorry."

"So, *that's* the reason I can see you?" Felix understood it all clearly now. "It's not fate. I'm not special. I can see you because I'm a—" He stopped short.

"You're a wish," Rupus confirmed.

"You've been *lying* to me this whole time?"

"Please, Felix. It's not quite like that. Please, take a seat. This must be such a shock." The elderly wishkeeper's eyes were wide and pleading.

Felix remained standing. His whole life felt like a balloon that could pop at any moment. *He wasn't real. He was a wish.* A silly wish that Rebecca had made as a little girl. She'd probably regretted it ever since.

It all made sense now. This was the reason he felt so useless and out of place at home. He didn't really belong there. He never had.

"I'm leaving," Felix said, stumbling towards the front door.

"You can't go. I need your help!" Rupus shouted, rushing into the hallway after him.

"You don't *deserve* my help," Felix shot back. "You got yourself into this mess by granting *illegal* wishes!"

The two of them, boy and wishkeeper, stood in silence. They were only a few metres apart, but, to Felix, it felt like a gulf had opened in the space between them.

"I – I only ever tried to help people." Rupus's voice was a half-whisper. "I never meant any harm. And…" He paused. "I never intended to put you in mortal danger."

Mortal danger.

Felix turned to face Rupus as a fresh realization hit him. "Wait! If – if I'm a wish, does that mean the wishsnatcher will destroy me?" In his gut, he already knew the answer.

"I'm so sorry, Felix. But, yes, it's only a matter of time before it tries." Rupus's brow was furrowed with guilt. "That's why I'm going to insist that you take the vanquisher home with you. You need protection."

The elderly wishkeeper lifted the tank from the hallway floor and placed it at Felix's feet. "I hope you won't need it. I hope it doesn't come to that. But I think it's best that you keep this by your side, just in case. Particularly after dark."

Felix eyed the small tank with doubt. "What about you?" he asked.

"I'll make sure to always be home by sundown." Rupus paused. "You should have the vanquisher, Felix. I'm the one who has put us both in danger."

110

Felix hesitated. He didn't know what to do. But the sense of betrayal at discovering that Rupus had lied to him was overwhelming. He'd begun to see Rupus as a friend. Felix had almost trusted that he might be of some use to someone. But that was all gone now.

Angrily, he reached out and took the heavy tank. His knees buckled under its weight.

"I'm going home now," he said, even though part of him felt like he didn't have a real home any more. All he knew was that he didn't want to be around Rupus.

He left without looking back.

13
The Wishsnatcher Strikes

Felix arrived home to an empty house.

The rest of his family was still visiting his grandparents. He lugged the vanquisher upstairs and lay on his bed, staring at a cluster of glow-in-the-dark stickers on his ceiling. He and his dad had put them up last summer. The memory felt like a lifetime ago.

Suddenly, Felix's entire ten years' worth of memories felt distant. It was as if his whole life was a kite, and he was only holding onto it by the thinnest of strings.

Felix remembered the charred remains of the

Half Moon Theatre. If the wishsnatcher found him and the vanquisher didn't work, would he meet a similar fate? Would he be burned to nothing?

He sat up quickly and read the instructions on the back of the metal tank. The first thing he noticed was the expiry date: *1975*. Felix's heart sank.

The contents list didn't give him much confidence either. The device claimed to contain a blend of "positive emotions" such as "stubborn hope" and "glints of joy", all of which were said to be carbonated. In addition, there was an allergy warning regarding flower pollen and a note that there "may be traces of cinnamon". Rupus had assured him that the vanquisher was a powerful weapon capable of destroying the wishsnatcher. But maybe that was just another lie?

Felix stared out of his window. The winter afternoon light was fading already. Felix wondered

if Rupus had received a reply from The Council of the Wishkeepers yet, and then shook the concern from his mind. Why should he be worrying about Rupus? Rupus was the one who had put him in mortal danger. Rupus was the one who had been lying to him this whole time. He was done helping Rupus. It was time to focus on protecting himself.

Felix hid the vanquisher in his wardrobe and climbed back into bed.

There was a quiet knock on the door, followed by his mum's voice as she opened it a crack. "Feeling any better, love?"

It took Felix a moment to remember that he was supposed to be ill. That was the excuse he'd used for skipping the family visit.

"Not really, no," Felix replied.

"You stay in bed, then," she said, looking down at him. He was spread out morosely on top of his bedspread. "Did you want something to eat? I saw you didn't eat the soup I left out for your lunch. I can make you a sandwich for dinner later."

"I'll come down and eat with you," Felix told her. He was keen for some company.

"Sorry, love, your dad and I have that charity dinner this evening." Felix's mum paused before adding, "But I think Rebecca is having some friends over for takeaway, if you feel well enough to join them?"

"Um, I'll pass," Felix replied, but his mum was already calling Rebecca upstairs.

Rebecca traipsed up the staircase and onto the landing.

"I was thinking Felix could join you and your pals this evening," Felix's mum suggested cheerily as if she expected Rebecca to be charmed by the idea.

"I thought you said you were *ill*." Rebecca raised an eyebrow at Felix.

"I am ill," Felix asserted. "I'm staying in bed."

"OK, that's decided, then," Rebecca said with a shrug before disappearing into her bedroom.

"Felix." His mum sighed. "You really don't help yourself sometimes."

"I know when I'm not wanted," Felix told her.

* * *

Hours later, after a very unsatisfying cheese-and-pickle sandwich, Felix hunted out his hand-held torch and sat up in bed, keeping watch from the window. He positioned the vanquisher by his side and pulled the duvet up to his neck. But despite his best intentions to stay awake, it wasn't long before his heavy eyelids closed and he fell into a restless sleep.

Felix was wrapped not in a duvet but in darkness. It was a cold, damp darkness. It crept under the neck of his pyjamas and made him shudder.

He peered around, trying to see where he was. This was a dream, but it felt eerily real. Someone was quite close, almost within touching distance, but behind a veil of night.

Felix realized he was under the railway bridge.

A growling voice broke from the shadows in front of him. "Where are we?"

"Silver Way," Felix replied. The words were out of his lips before he'd had a chance to think.

Suddenly, he remembered his promise to keep Snugwarm's address a secret. It was the most important secret he'd ever been trusted with and he'd just given it away.

Felix felt a panic growing inside him and a desire to get away from the voice. He ran his hands along the brick wall, looking for the door to Rupus's house. If he could get inside, he would be safe. He felt the smooth metal of the door knocker under his fingertips. In the faint light, he could just about make out a brass number.

"Tell me the number," the voice hissed.

"No."

"Tell me," the voice insisted.

Felix felt a heavy paw on his shoulder. Claws dug into his collarbone. Felix gasped.

"Is this a dream?" he asked.

"Yes. It will be over soon," the voice told him. "Now, tell me the number."

Felix could feel ice-cold breath on the back of his neck. The claws tore through his shoulder muscles to the bone.

Felix screamed in pain.

He didn't want to speak, but he couldn't keep the words inside. "One." Felix's legs buckled under him and he fell to his knees. "Four." He writhed in agony under the creature's grip. "Three." He screamed the last syllable.

Two red eyes shone out of the dark…

Felix woke with a jolt, still clutching the vanquisher. The image of the red eyes lingered in his mind.

Deep in his gut, he knew it hadn't just been a dream. The monster from his nightmares was the wishsnatcher. The creature was real, and it was as awful as Rupus had described.

A torrent of fear ran through Felix. If that monster got its hands on Rupus, then every wish in Whittlestone would be destroyed for ever, and Rupus would be destroyed along with them. Felix had to get to Rupus before it was too late.

Felix was wearing nothing more than his pyjamas as he hauled his bicycle out from the shed.

He had no idea of the time, but it was still dark. He placed the vanquisher securely in the front basket and leaped onto the seat. Under the light of the streetlamps, Felix raced as fast as he could, soaring along the empty roads towards Rupus's house.

The sky was pitch-black, and it was pouring with rain. By the time he got to the market square, he was soaked through. Then something strange happened.

One minute Felix was on the bike, the next second he was hurtling through the air. He landed, arms first, in the middle of the road. The tarmac ripped into his elbow and his head came down hard with a crack.

For an instant, Felix lay still, frozen in shock.

Eventually, he hoisted himself up into a seated position. His bicycle was nowhere to be seen, but at his feet was an open umbrella.

"What on earth?" He looked around for the bike and saw two more umbrellas lying crumpled under the metal frame of a coat stand. Felix remembered what Rupus had said about making his treasured bike out of umbrellas and a coat stand.

The wishsnatcher had snatched another wish.

14
The Council of the Wishkeepers

It was dawn by the time Felix finally arrived at Silver Way. He staggered as quickly as he could towards the railway bridge, cradling the heavy vanquisher, which now sported a large dent. A terrible headache pounded behind his bruised forehead, but Felix tried his best to stay focused. He'd been much slower on foot than he would have been on his bike. He only hoped he had made it in time.

The front door in the brick wall was ajar. Felix's heart sank like a stone. He couldn't imagine

Rupus leaving the door open while there was a wishsnatcher about.

Felix looked despairingly into the dark cavity behind the door. *Please be here, Rupus. Please be OK.* He pointed the nozzle of the vanquisher into the hallway as he inched forward.

Snugwarm had never felt less snug. A sensation of dread repelled him. Felix longed to get away, but he couldn't give up on his friend. He pressed onwards.

Something crunched below his feet. In the dim gloom, he could just about make out a broken mirror on the floor. Deep claw marks were scratched into the floorboards beside it. Felix shuddered.

"Rupus!" he shouted. "Rupus, it's me, Felix! Are you here?"

There was no answer. The final drops of remaining hope drained away.

Rupus was gone.

This was all his fault. He had betrayed Rupus's secret. He had led the wishsnatcher straight to Rupus's door.

Felix set down the vanquisher and crumpled into Rupus's desk chair. He looked at the old-fashioned wishofax machine on the desk in front of him. Felix had no idea how the messaging machine worked, but he needed to get help fast. Then he noticed a letter sticking out of it. Rupus must not have had a chance to read it.

Dear Rupus,

Thank you for your most recent correspondence. On the behalf of The Council, I would like to reassure you that wishsnatchers no longer exist. Our records indicate that the last and final wishnatcher was destroyed in 1973.

In future, please only send emergency messages to this line.

Any further queries you have should be directed to our general enquiries line on 825693. Please note there is a two- to three-week wait time for general enquiries.

Yours sincerely,

Benjamin Tumble

Communications Manager

The Council of the Wishkeepers

Felix crumpled the page in frustration and threw the ball of paper to the floor. The Council of the Wishkeepers didn't believe them.

Felix sat down at the machine and typed a note angrily.

URGENT MESSAGE FOR THE COUNCIL OF THE WISHKEEPERS

A wishsnatcher HAS attacked Whittlestone. Rupus Beewinkle has been captured.

You should have believed him!

If anyone at the Council cares at all about Whittlestone, then please send help immediately.

From,

Felix Jones (Rupus's apprentice)

There was no point waiting on a response. The Council was useless.

Felix tapped his fingertips anxiously. Right now, somewhere out there, a wishsnatcher was extracting wishes from Rupus's soul and obliterating them one by one. It was only a matter of time before Rupus and all his wishes, including Felix, were gone. There was no time to hang about. Felix was on his own, and if he didn't act soon, there would be nothing left to save.

Felix threw on one of Rupus's overcoats and grabbed a large satchel from a hook by the front door. He shoved the vanquisher inside and slung it over his shoulder.

As he was leaving the room, he noticed something else lying on the moth-eaten carpet. It was a small brass disc. Felix recognized the object instantly. He'd often seen Rupus fidgeting with it. He'd assumed it was a pocket watch. A single

word was etched into the brass lid: *Wishometer*. He opened it. Inside, Felix found not a clock face but a dial. It read: *01343*.

As he considered it, the number changed to 01342. Then it changed again, to 01341, and then 01340. The dial was going backwards.

Suddenly, Felix understood what he was looking at. It was a device for counting wishes. He was watching Rupus Beewinkle's wishes disappear and Rupus with them. There was no time to spare.

15
Regina Blackbird's Missing Wish

F elix knew he'd never make it to the coal mines on foot in time to save Rupus. He had no choice but to confide in someone. He could always count on his family when he really needed them. Even Rebecca. All he wanted was a lift, after all.

Hang in there, Rupus, Felix thought as he hurried towards home carrying the heavy vanquisher.

As he passed the square, Regina Blackbird the baker was opening up. Felix did a double take when he saw the sign above the shop. It read:

WASH & GO

Washing/drying/ironing services
available here

The cosy bakery with its array of pastries and squidgy armchairs was gone. In its place was a bare room with two benches and a dozen washing machines. Regina Blackbird was dressed in a bright-orange apron emblazoned with the *Wash & Go* logo.

Felix shook his head. "It's supposed to be a bakery," he half-whispered, staring in disbelief at the garish sign above the shop front.

"A bakery?" Regina raised an eyebrow and dusted off her apron. Her hands were calloused and sore from soap suds. "I wish," she added.

"Yes!" Felix's heart was thudding. "You *did* wish."

His bicycle was gone. The bakery was gone. How many other wishes had been snatched from Rupus's soul already?

Felix tightened his grip on the vanquisher and walked faster.

When Felix finally rounded the corner onto the street where he lived, he saw his mum and dad in the driveway, scraping ice off the windscreen of the car. No doubt they were heading out to search for him after finding his bed empty that morning.

He rushed towards them. "Hey!"

"Are you OK?" Felix's dad asked.

Felix's chest heaved as he took a few gulps of air, only now realizing how dishevelled he must look.

"That looks serious," said Felix's mum, nodding at the graze on Felix's elbow. It had happened when he fell off the bike. "Do you need us to call someone?"

"No. I don't need a doctor or anything. I just need—"

His mum cut him off. "Let's get you some antiseptic." She led him through the front door and into the kitchen. "Ouch. I bet that hurt?" she said as Felix flinched when she peeled back the torn fabric of his jumper and pyjama shirt to inspect his elbow.

"It's not too bad," he reassured her. "Listen, I need to tell you something." Felix had no idea where to begin. Would they even believe him? They had to believe him. How else was he going to get to the coal mines in time to save Rupus?

"It looks painful to me," his mum insisted, pursing her lips. "I really think we should call someone for you." She glanced at Felix's pyjama bottoms and soggy trainers. "Oh dear, you are in a mess. Nick!" she called. "Nick, could you bring the phone through?" Felix noticed she was speaking in her "very polite" voice. It was a bit weird. Maybe she and his dad had had an argument, or something.

Felix's dad emerged from the hallway with the

phone. "Everything OK?"

"He's got a bad graze. Nothing too serious, but that freezing fog isn't going anywhere and no one wants to be out in that if they don't need to be." She glanced out of the window. "What's the number, dear?"

The question was directed at Felix.

"What do you mean?" Felix asked. He looked from his mum to his dad and back again. Their expressions were neutral and puzzled, as if Felix had asked a silly question.

"What's your parents' phone number?" his mum asked. "We need to let them know you are here."

Felix stumbled backwards. His sore elbow crashed against the kitchen worktop, but he was so shaken that he didn't even feel the impact.

Both of his parents were staring at him with expressions of worry, but he was suddenly aware that it wasn't the right kind of worry. This was

the type of concern shown by kind strangers. The man and woman in front of him hadn't spent the morning searching desperately for their missing son. They had no idea who he was.

"No. This can't be happening," Felix whispered. His parents had forgotten him.

"We can give you a lift, if that's easier?" his dad offered. "We were just about to drive to work. Do you live near by?"

16
The Photo on the Mantelpiece

Without a word, Felix darted out of the kitchen. He crossed the hallway and burst into the living room. His eyes shot straight to the mantelpiece, where a large family portrait of the four of them stood proudly. Except there weren't four people in the photograph. Now, there were only three: Mum, Dad and Rebecca.

Felix fought back tears as he raced up the stairs in a last-ditch attempt to dispel his fears. He grasped the door handle to his bedroom, and the door swung open with a familiar creak.

The first thing Felix  ought to have seen was his bookshelf, packed neatly with books. Next to that should have been his bed and a stack of comics. Instead, his eyes surveyed a sparsely furnished room that contained nothing but a treadmill and a rowing machine.

"The loo is at the end of the landing," his dad called from below.

Felix felt numb.

Suddenly, Rebecca's bedroom door opened. She stood in the doorway and looked him up and down. She was still in her dressing gown and pyjamas. Behind her, loud rock music was blaring out of a pair of speakers.

"Who are *you*?" she asked, folding her arms.

Felix didn't reply. Instead, he held her gaze and

willed her to recognize him. *It's me, Rebecca. It's Felix. Please tell me you know who I am.*

"Dad!" Rebecca shouted. "There's a kid up here on the landing."

"Yes, we know, love," Felix's mum explained patiently from the hallway. "He's just using the loo."

Suddenly, Rebecca's expression changed from confusion to horror. Felix followed her gaze to the floor and felt a jolt of panic.

Both of his feet had disappeared. His pyjama-bottomed legs were hovering in mid-air. Instinctively, he stretched out his hands to touch his feet to check they were still there, even if not visible. To his horror, his hands flickered, disappearing and reappearing.

Rebecca's eyebrows contorted to give her an expression of pure terror. "Mum! Dad!" she yelled.

Felix turned and dashed down the stairs in a hurricane of panic. He slammed the front door

behind him as he stumbled into the pelting rain and fog outside.

His mind raced. The three people who knew him better than anyone else had no idea who he was.

He had been obliterated. He no longer existed.

As the rain soaked through his clothes, Felix looked down and saw his feet flickering back into view and then disappearing again.

He felt the squelch of water inside his trainers and the icy cold rain tricking down his neck. Somehow, he was still here. But for how much longer?

A flash of blue caught his eye, and Felix looked across the street to see the number 12 bus about to depart. It was heading in the right direction for the coal mines. He saw his chance and dashed forward, leaping through the door just in time.

Fortunately, there were a few pennies in the pocket of Rupus's coat. Felix stretched his palm out, hoping that they might magically transform into the two pounds thirty fare he needed. But they remained as pennies.

The bus driver gave him a sympathetic look before taking the handful of coins. "Nobody should be walking to school in this weather," she said with a kind smile.

Felix found a seat at the back of the bus, making himself as inconspicuous as he could. Hopefully the

other passengers wouldn't notice that he was semi-transparent.

Felix stared out of the rain-battered window, feeling utterly lost. It would take half an hour to get to the outskirts of town and he'd have to walk to the coal mines from there. Poor Rupus. Would he be able to wait that long?

Then a panicked thought bolted into his mind: the vanquisher! He'd left it at home. He couldn't go to the coal mines without it. He wouldn't stand a chance against the wishsnatcher.

"Stop the bus!" Felix shouted.

Half a dozen passengers turned to look at him. The driver pulled in and gave him a look of concern. "Everything OK?" she asked.

Felix didn't reply. He bolted through the open door. A car's horn blasted as he crossed the road, barely looking where he was going.

Felix watched the bus pull away. He was miles

from home. How could he have been so stupid as to forget the vanquisher?

The sound of another horn blasted from behind him. Felix stepped off the road onto the pavement, but the beeping continued. Eventually, he turned around.

A familiar yellow Volvo had emerged from the fog and pulled in at the side of the road. Felix stared in disbelief at the wide-eyed girl in the driver's seat. She rolled the window down.

"Hey," she shouted. "Hey, you there!"

17
The Yellow Volvo

"Rebecca?"

Felix moved hesitantly towards the car. *Why was she here? How had she found him? Had she remembered who he was?*

"How do you know my name?" Rebecca asked suspiciously through the open car window.

"Oh," Felix replied. "So, you don't know who I am, then?"

"I know *what* you are," Rebecca answered, looking at him intently. "I have your fire extinguisher, by the way."

"What? How – how did you find me?"

"I saw you get on the bus. I know the route so I followed you."

"What?" Felix shook his head in disbelief. "Why would you do that?"

"Well, you ran off so suddenly and you forgot your bag." Rebecca shrugged. "I figured it might be important."

"Yes. It's *really* important," Felix replied, feeling a wave of relief at the sight of the vanquisher on the passenger seat beside her.

He couldn't believe his luck. Rebecca wasn't usually the type for acts of kindness. But, thanks to her, he stood a chance of saving Rupus. It was a small chance, but it was a chance.

"Could you give me a lift somewhere?" he asked, hoping he wasn't pushing his luck.

To his surprise, Rebecca nodded enthusiastically. "Sure! Hop in."

Felix clambered into the passenger side and

clutched the vanquisher to his chest. "I can't believe you came after me."

"Well, what can I say? I didn't want to miss my chance to meet a real-life ghost."

"What do you mean, a ghost? Oh." Felix suddenly understood her mistake. Of course Rebecca would think he was a ghost. He was semi-transparent and she'd watched every supernatural film in existence.

"So, am I right?" his sister asked. Her enthusiasm was palpable. "Are you a ghost?"

"Um, yes, I suppose I am a *sort* of ghost," Felix replied honestly. "I'm not real any more. But I'm not completely gone either."

"I see." Rebecca nodded, as if this made complete sense. "It's probably because you have unfinished business."

"Right," Felix replied.

"Maybe I can help you?" Rebecca gave him a

sympathetic smile as she inspected his translucent hands. "Can you see a bright light anywhere?"

Felix recognized the question from one of Rebecca's favourite ghost-hunting documentaries. He almost smiled with amusement, but then he remembered the task ahead of him. Rupus's life was in danger. Felix's own existence hung in the balance, and so did the existence of thousands of other wishes.

"Do you know the way to the coal mines?" he asked, changing the subject and turning his attention to the journey ahead.

"I think so," Rebecca replied.

"Can you take me there?"

"OK. Are you going to tell me why?"

Felix hesitated. He was going to need to come up with some kind of an explanation. "It's a secret," he said. "I have to sort out my unfinished business."

"I see." Rebecca nodded before casting him a sideways look. "Are you *actually* putting on a seat belt? Aren't you already dead?"

"Force of habit, I guess." Felix shrugged as he clicked the seat belt into place. He wasn't taking any risks with Rebecca's driving.

"This is so cool," Rebecca said. "My film club is going to go crazy when I tell them about this."

"I'm glad to provide a good anecdote," Felix replied unenthusiastically.

"So, what's with the extinguisher?" Rebecca nodded at the vanquisher inside the satchel.

Felix was clinging to it like a lifebuoy. The thought of his imminent encounter with the wishsnatcher was making him feel faint. He remembered the wolf-man's snarling smile. What were the chances of the vanquisher actually working?

"Again, I can't tell you that. I'm sorry. It's to do with my unfinished business, you see."

"I see." Rebecca sighed. They stopped at a red light. She popped open the glove box and reached in for a bag of gummy bears.

Felix recognized the packaging immediately. Goldilocks Drops had been his and Rebecca's favourite sweets ever since they were little.

"Want one?" His sister offered him the bag.

Felix felt a wave of sadness as the familiar sugary smell filled the car.

Rebecca glanced at him as he choked back tears. "Oh, sorry. I guess ghosts can't eat."

"No, it's not that. I can eat." He reached into the bag and pulled out a ruby-coloured bear. Strawberry. Those were his favourite. He remembered how Rebecca had always given him her strawberry bears in exchange for his orange ones.

"I'm starving. I haven't had breakfast," Rebecca said.

Felix had never known Rebecca to skip a meal. She was clearly dedicated to ghost-hunting. He picked out a few orange sweets and passed them to her as she drove.

It was surprisingly reassuring to be in Rebecca's company, even though she had no idea who he was. The familiarity of the car and the sweets were a welcome distraction from the task ahead. Felix chewed quietly before Rebecca broke the silence again.

"I've just remembered something," she said. "We had some history lessons at college about the coal mines." She paused. "They used to send child workers down there." She left the statement hanging for a moment. "I think it's terrible that they did that."

Felix saw where she was going with this. Clearly, she'd decided he was a coal-mining ghost. He looked down at his torn, dirty clothes. "Yes, it was really awful." He sighed dramatically. "Horribly dark and sooty. I'd rather not talk about it."

"Yes, of course." Rebecca bit her lip. "Sorry I brought that up."

The two of them sat in an awkward silence as Rebecca drove the final stretch to the coal mines. Eventually, they pulled in at the side of the road.

"Is this close enough?" she asked.

Felix peered down the country lane that led to the old abandoned mines. Thick fog clouded the way. He didn't blame her for not wanting to drive any further.

"Yes. Thanks, this is fine." He handed her the half-empty bag of Goldilocks Drops.

"No, you keep them," she insisted. "You look hungry."

Felix gratefully stashed the sweets in his back pocket and reached for a torch that he'd spotted in the glove box. "I need to borrow this," he told her. "Could you wait here for me to come back?"

Rebecca nodded.

"I might be a while."

"I'll wait," Rebecca told him. "I'm only missing business studies."

Suddenly, a fresh thought hit Felix. He might not ever come back from the mines.

"If I come back," Felix said, "I'll just need a lift to town again. I might have a friend with me, but … well, he's invisible, so you won't see him. And if I don't come back…" He met Rebecca's eye and felt a lump in his throat. "If I don't come back, then that just means I've finally sorted out my unfinished business." He forced a smile. "So, don't be worried about me. I'll have moved on – you know, into the light."

Rebecca nodded earnestly. "Good luck, ghost

boy!" she called after him as he stepped out of the car into the freezing fog.

Felix slung the satchel over his shoulder and fixed his gaze ahead. The pathway to the coal mines looked otherworldly in the grey daylight.

If I have to die, Felix thought, *then this is the best way.* This way Rebecca and his parents would never miss him. He'd be no more than a spooky story shared from time to time at the dinner table.

He turned to give Rebecca one last look. She was leaning out of the open window of the car, giving him a brave smile and a thumbs-up. He'd never seen her looking more big-sisterly than she did in that moment.

18
Into the Coal Mines

Getting into the abandoned colliery was a challenge. The obvious entrance had been roped off and barricaded with boards to prevent hooligans venturing in. It took Felix ages to find another way through.

Eventually, he sensed the all-too-familiar scent of despair in the air and followed the trail to the mouth of a tunnel. Most of the entrance had been bricked up, but there was a gap large enough for Felix to squeeze through.

Felix checked the wishometer again. The dial was oscillating between 0001 and 0000. Felix

inspected his own flickering hands. He was half-here and half-gone. Rupus Beewinkle was clinging onto his most illegal wish by a thread. Felix's entire existence hung in the balance.

"I'm coming, Rupus," Felix whispered into the darkness of the tunnel. "Hang in there."

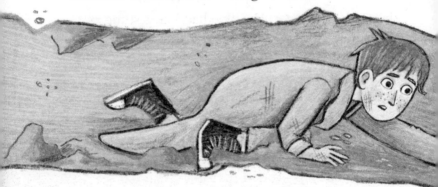

Felix pulled the vanquisher out and thrust the empty satchel to the ground. Then he shuffled forward on his hands and knees, pushing the vanquisher ahead of him. The ground was uneven and stony. Felix wished he were wearing something a bit more hard-wearing than his pyjama bottoms.

After a short distance, the tunnel opened into a black chasm of darkness. Felix got to his feet, clutching the vanquisher in one hand and reaching for the torch in his pocket with the other. He didn't want to turn it on, in case the light alerted the wishsnatcher, but it was comforting to know it was there if he needed it. His bloodied knees stung as his eyes slowly adjusted to the gloom.

"Who's there?" said a growling voice in the distance. "I can hear you breathing."

Felix shrank back. He could sense the wishsnatcher approaching, but he had no idea how

close it was. He gripped the vanquisher tightly, scrabbling to find the nozzle. He needed to hold his nerve until the creature was within range.

Felix held out his torch and turned it on. The light revealed an awful wolfish creature, standing upright on its two hind legs. It was ten metres away, and its red eyes were staring straight at him. It was the monster from his nightmares. Except this time, it was for real.

"Felix Jones. I thought you might come." The wishsnatcher smiled a horrible smile. "It isn't a dream this time. You won't wake up from this."

"Where is Rupus?" Felix demanded, wielding the extinguisher like a sword. He tried his best to remain focused as the smell of despair engulfed him. "What have you done with him?" Felix's voice cracked.

The wishsnatcher scoffed. "Oh dear. You didn't get attached to little old Rupus, did you? Rupus

Beewinkle is gone for ever. Just like his wishes. Just like you."

The wolfish creature was only a few metres away. It was walking on all fours with its jaw stretched into a wide, toothy grin.

"Take one more step and I will destroy you!" Felix shook with fear and rage as he raised the vanquisher.

A guttural laugh rose from the wishsnatcher's throat. "You? Destroy me? You can't destroy me. You can't do anything, Felix Jones. You're not real. You never were. You were only ever a wish."

19

The Vanquisher

"*I* am real," Felix said, but his voice sounded quiet and far away. "I am real," he said again.

Felix dropped the lit torch and grasped the nozzle of the vanquisher. His flickering hands disappeared completely for a moment, and Felix froze.

The wishsnatcher gave a horrible cackle and stood on its hind legs. "You are nothing more than a wish and I *will* destroy you." It swiped at him with its claws.

Felix ducked just in time, but he felt the pocket on Rupus's overcoat tear. There was a clink as

the wishometer fell to the tunnel floor. As Felix stumbled to reach for it in the dark, he dropped the vanquisher and it rolled away. He fumbled in the half-darkness to find it. Just as the wishsnatcher reached him, he managed to pull the trigger.

The force of the jet knocked the wind from Felix's chest. He gasped and tightened his grip, directing the full force of the blast into the wishsnatcher's beastly face until there was nothing left in the container.

The wishsnatcher let out a howl. There was a heavy thump as the monster's body fell to the ground. Felix picked up his torch and summoned all his courage to take a closer look.

The wishsnatcher's eyes were closed. Bravely, Felix lowered his cheek to the creature's still open jaw. He could feel the creature's breath rising and falling. His heart sank. The vanquisher hadn't been enough. The wishsnatcher was still alive.

"Is that all you've got, Felix?" the wishsnatcher grunted. Felix leaped back and the wishsnatcher knocked the empty vanquisher from his hands. The tank bounced and rolled away into the darkness.

Felix's mind went blank with panic. He was completely defenceless.

The wishsnatcher groaned and rolled onto all fours. It grabbed the gold wishometer from the ground and flicked it open with a single claw.

"Only one more wish remaining!" it sang gleefully. Its face was contorted into a snarling grin. Its red eyes shone with victory. "One wish to destroy and then Whittlestone is all mine."

Felix felt a wave of despair crash through his body, but he refused to give in to it. It wasn't over yet. He knew he couldn't outrun the creature, but maybe he could hide.

He grasped the torch and turned on the spot, sprinting down the tunnel that led deeper into the mine, as the wishsnatcher gave chase.

Ahead, the single tunnel split into three smaller openings. Felix turned his torch off and ducked into one of them at random. His only hope was that the wishsnatcher would choose a different tunnel. That would buy him some time. Felix froze in the darkness, waiting to see what would happen.

There was a noise close by.

"Show yourself!" the creature screamed.

Felix picked up a small stone and launched it into the air, throwing it at a different opening. Felix held his breath and listened until he heard the sound of the wishsnatcher's claws as it headed in the direction of the noise, away from where Felix was hiding.

Felix exhaled and turned his torch back on to get his bearings. He was in a small cavelike space,

with jagged walls. The torchlight flitted around the cave as Felix's hand shook. He gasped as the circle of light revealed a crumpled figure on the floor.

"Rupus?" Felix whispered in disbelief.

The elderly wishkeeper had his head tucked below his arm, like a sleeping bird. Felix lifted it to reveal broken spectacles and limp whiskers hanging on an ashen face. Rupus's eyes were closed, but Felix noticed his whiskers move as he took a shallow breath. Rupus was still alive. Felix felt his spirits soar. It wasn't over yet. They could still escape. They could still save Whittlestone.

He set the torch down quietly and grasped

Rupus's forearms. He pulled with all his might, heaving the wishkeeper's frail body through the neck of the cave and into the tunnel beyond.

The darkness was overwhelming, but Felix fixed his gaze on the faint grey light ahead. Somewhere within himself, he mustered the strength to drag Rupus all the way to the tunnel entrance.

But the wishsnatcher wasn't done with them yet. "Give yourself up!" came its voice from somewhere behind them. "I *will* find you."

Trying to ignore his fear and panic, Felix pushed Rupus's limp body through the narrow opening of the mines before scrambing out after him. Daylight illuminated the desolate yard.

Felix scanned the surroundings. It was no good. There was nowhere for them to hide.

"Felix?" Rupus croaked, squinting in the light. "You came."

"Of course—" Felix began. But before he could

say another word, he felt an ice-cold claw tear into his shoulder. The pain was blinding, and he was thrown head-first across the yard.

Felix's forehead smashed into the hard earth. For a few seconds, he lay perfectly still, feeling dazed before he mustered the strength to look up. To his horror, he saw the wishsnatcher standing over Rupus. The creature had dug a single claw into Rupus's matted cloud of hair and was pulling a shining copper thread from his scalp.

Suddenly Felix understood what he was seeing. The wishsnatcher was extracting the final wish from Rupus. Rebecca's wish.

"Hold on, Rupus!" Felix pleaded. "Hold on!"

One look at Rupus's face told him that Rupus didn't have the strength to hold on any longer. Felix's entire existence was about to be erased. This would be worse than dying. He would never have existed at all.

Rupus's grey-green eyes opened to meet Felix's desperate gaze. "I can't," he whispered. "I can't hold on any longer. Unless…" His eyes widened as one final thought occurred to him. "Take it, Felix," he said. "Snatch it!"

In an instant, Felix understood what Rupus was telling him to do.

Felix stared at the glittering thread. It was still rooted in Rupus's head, pulled taut by the wishsnatcher's grip. Icy despair filled Felix's heart as the wishsnatcher turned his horrible wolfish face towards him. The creature's empty eyes bore into him.

"Don't you dare," the wishsnatcher growled.

Felix felt an overwhelming desire to give up. What was the point? It was all over. Then Rupus gave one final whisper:

"I believe in you, Felix Jones."

Hope surged through Felix, and he managed to

tear his eyes away from the wishsnatcher's face. He fixed them on the copper thread.

One last try.

Felix pushed his weight onto his bloodied knees and launched himself at the final wish with an open and outstretched hand.

20
The Last Wish

*F*elix tumbled head-first and his fingers closed on the silky thread. He landed prostrate on the damp earth, gripping Rupus's final wish.

Suddenly, the grey fog around Felix was gone, replaced by crisp, clear sunlight. The ground had been transformed into cobblestones, and his ears were filled with the sound of hustle and bustle.

Felix blinked and looked up in bewilderment. Shoes, ankles and shopping bags swarmed around him. He clambered to his feet. This was Whittlestone's market square. A dozen shopping

stalls were up and open for business. It was market day.

He turned around on the spot. There was no sign of Rupus or the wishsnatcher.

He had done it. He had snatched the last wish. But what on earth was happening now?

"Rebecca, Rebecca!" came a frantic shout from the crowd.

Felix knew the voice instantly. It was his mum's. He scanned the faces in the crowd as a small girl charged straight into him.

"Sorry," said the girl without looking up as she dashed to the fountain's edge.

Felix watched her lean over to see the coins below.

"Oh, Rebecca, I was so *worried*." Felix's mum emerged from the swarm of people and placed a hand on the little girl's shoulder. For a moment, he didn't recognize her with her long wavy hair. He was used to seeing her with a short bob. But the point of her chin and the green of her eyes were the same.

Felix knew what he was seeing now. This was it. This was Rebecca's wish. This was the wish that had brought him into existence.

"It's all right, Nick. She's here," Felix's mum called.

Felix's dad burst through the crowd. The relief on his face was obvious. "How many times do we have to tell you, Rebecca?" he said. "You need to stay close. No running off when it's crowded."

"Sorry, Daddy," said little Rebecca. She looked up at her parents. "I just have a *brilliant* wish idea."

"What's that?" asked Felix's mum.

"I can't tell you or it won't come true." Rebecca stretched out her open hand. "Please, Daddy."

Felix's dad pulled some change from his pocket and handed her a penny. "I'm sure it's a great wish."

"The *best*," Rebecca told him as she squeezed her eyes shut. "The *bestest*, *best* wish ever."

She tossed her coin into the water with a splash and laughed. Felix felt her happiness ripple outwards. He saw the joy spread to his parents' faces. Then he felt his own face stretch into the same wide smile.

There was a tickling sensation in his hand. Felix looked down at the copper thread, which was coiling into a circle. A moment later, it had transformed into a shiny penny.

In an instant, Felix felt different. First, there was the feeling of returning home after a long absence. Next came a gentle warmth, accompanied by the scent of hot chocolate and cinnamon.

The tingling anticipation of birthdays and Christmas mornings filled the air. Felix took a few breaths until his mind jingled with presents, laughter and family. Hope kindled in his heart.

Then a sense of peace engulfed him, like the comfort of climbing into your own bed after a long day. In the same moment, the bright noon sunlight faded, and he was wrapped in grey fog.

21
The Wish Boy

*F*elix stared at the spot where his family had been just moments ago. In their place stood the wishsnatcher, still gripping the limp body of Rupus.

"You took it!" the wishsnatcher hissed. "You snatched the wish." His awful mouth contorted into a snarl as he threw an unconscious Rupus to one side.

Felix felt no fear now as he looked into the cold, empty eyes of the creature. He was still full to the brim with the joy of the wish memory. He had never been more certain of two things. Firstly, that

he was wanted. And, secondly, that he was loved. He had been loved since before he even existed. He had been *wished* for.

"Give it to me," the wishsnatcher snarled, baring his teeth.

Felix still felt no fear. "No," he replied simply.

And then he knew exactly what to do. He allowed the happiness in his heart to seep into his face. His mouth opened into another wide smile.

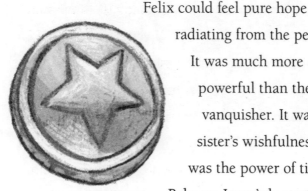

Felix could feel pure hope radiating from the penny. It was much more powerful than the vanquisher. It was his sister's wishfulness. It was the power of tiny Rebecca Jones's bestest, best wish. Felix held up the shining penny.

The wishsnatcher recoiled. It let out a long yowl

and turned away as if the sight of Felix was unbearable. Then it fled, disappearing into the tunnel.

Felix stood in silence for a moment and peered at the figure crumpled on the ground. The small frame of Rupus Beewinkle was curled up like a wounded animal.

"Rupus?" Felix took a step forward. "Rupus, it's OK. You're going to be all right now." He kneeled by the body of his friend. He lifted Rupus's hand, but it was stone cold.

Panic rose in Felix's chest. Every last wish had been snatched from Rupus's being. What did that mean? Was he dying? Was he *dead*?

Suddenly, a blare of light came out of nowhere. Felix squinted as he turned his face to see two bright circles coming straight at him. Fog lights.

"Hey, ghost boy. Everything OK?" Rebecca shouted as she stepped out of the driver's side of the car.

Felix couldn't believe his eyes. Rebecca was

coming to his rescue for the second time that day. Maybe she wasn't such a terrible big sister, after all.

"I need a lift," Felix shouted. He had no idea if Rupus would survive, but he needed to get him out of the cold. They could get back to Snugwarm in fifteen minutes in a car. Felix heaved Rupus's body from the ground.

To his horror, as Felix carried him towards the car, Rupus's face began to sprout fur. Felix dropped him in shock.

Long fangs hung in Rupus's open mouth, and now his stubby fingers grew razor-sharp talons. Felix shook his head in disbelief. It looked like… It couldn't be… Rupus was transforming into a *wishsnatcher*. How was that possible?

Rebecca stood by the car, oblivious to the invisible wolf-man metres away from her. Felix looked back at Rupus, just as his eyelids opened to reveal piercing red eyes.

"Get back in the car!" Felix shouted to Rebecca. "Now!"

When she didn't move, he hurtled towards her, shoving her through the open car door. She tumbled over the driver's seat, knocking the handbrake as she scrambled awkwardly into the passenger seat, with Felix next to her.

Felix slammed the door behind him and pulled the handbrake back up, to stop the car from rolling.

Rupus Beewinkle was in full view, caught in the car's headlights. He was unrecognizable. The once feeble wishkeeper had grown a metre taller and was covered in monstrous fur.

"Lock the doors!" Felix yelled.

Rebecca jolted into action, and there was a series of reassuring clicks, although Felix doubted the car would provide much protection. Something told him that the little Volvo wouldn't be much of a match for Rupus's new claws.

"What on earth is going on?" Rebecca asked.

He could hear that she was spooked.

"There's a ferocious monster out there."

Rebecca stared wide-eyed at the unseen monster.

Meanwhile, Rupus had grabbed a rock. He hurled it at the windscreen. Rebecca screamed as the glass cracked with the impact. Felix couldn't remember ever seeing her look so afraid. He had to do something. He couldn't let his sister get hurt, not when it was her wish that had saved him. She had

given him the courage and the hope he'd needed to stand up to the wishsnatcher.

"No!" Felix shouted at the top of his lungs. He popped the lock on his door and opened it a crack so that Rupus could hear him. "Not her! It's me you want."

"Are you mad?!" Rebecca screeched. "Shut the door. There's something out there!"

"I know, but it's OK. The monster wants me. Not you. If I get out, it will leave you alone."

"But we can drive!" she said. "Let's get out of here now."

"No," Felix replied. "It's no good. The monster won't give up. He'll follow us. He'll find us. I can't risk you getting hurt too." Felix stared at Rupus in disbelief. He was truly monstrous. Felix felt his heart sink like a stone. The old Rupus was gone – probably for ever. And there was no way Felix could risk leading another wishsnatcher into

Whittlestone. It would endanger everyone he loved. No, enough damage had been done already. He was the last remaining wish. If he handed himself over, then at least that might be the end of it.

"But I don't want *you* to get hurt," Rebecca insisted. Her eyes were the wide eyes Felix remembered from his early childhood. The same eyes that had pleaded with him so many times not to go *too high* up in the tree, not to go *too fast* down the hill, not to go *too deep* into the waves.

Felix wished he could put her mind at rest, but he was already in far too deep. There was no going back now. Another rock crashed into the windscreen. There was no way out. All he could do was save Rebecca.

"Don't worry," Felix said. "I can't get hurt." He gave Rebecca a reassuring smile. "I'm already a ghost, remember?"

Felix grabbed the car keys from the dashboard

and launched himself out of the car. He slammed the door shut and locked Rebecca in from the outside. He couldn't risk her trying to get out to follow him. He'd never forgive himself if she got hurt.

Felix could hear the thuds of Rebecca hammering on the car window. But he didn't turn back. Instead, he fixed his eyes on the figure of the awful creature that had once been his friend. Every trace of the old Rupus was gone.

"I know you are going to destroy me." Felix's voice broke with emotion. "But, please, promise me one thing. Don't let her see it." He swallowed hard. "And don't hurt her."

"OK," the monster replied. His voice was cold and cruel. Rupus Beewinkle's whimsical tone was gone, but Felix noticed his red eyes narrow, as if he was puzzled. "You – you came out of the car … to protect her?"

"Yes," Felix replied.

There was a long paused before Rupus the wishsnatcher eventually said, "That was *kind*."

Felix watched in amazement as the creature let out a great sigh and scratched his head with a long talon. Then, suddenly, without warning, the monstrous Rupus sat down cross-legged on the muddy ground, like a confused child.

22
Goldilocks Drops

"Aren't you going to destroy me?" Felix asked. He was still vaguely aware of the thuds behind him as Rebecca hammered on the car window.

"Yes. Yes, of course I am," Monster Rupus said, still sitting on the ground. "I am a wishsnatcher and we do what we do." He frowned and gave a little snarl of frustration. "And what we do is destroy wishes."

"So, you *are* going to destroy me?"

"I might just leave it for now," he replied. "I'm feeling a bit confused. Maybe I'll destroy you another time."

"OK," Felix replied. He couldn't believe it.

"I'm going to go back to the cave," Monster Rupus said, getting to his feet. "It's dark there and I like it." He pulled off the broken spectacles and threw them to the ground.

Felix stared at the round frames and remembered the kind face of his friend.

"No," Felix shouted, as Rupus began to tread slowly to the tunnel opening. "Don't go!"

The furred face turned towards him. There was something very wolfish about the nose and mouth, but the red eyes had faded. In their place was a pair of wide, bewildered grey-green eyes.

"Rupus!" Felix exclaimed. "Rupus, you're still in there!"

"No. No, that's not right." Rupus looked rather alarmed. He shook his head rapidly and turned to leave.

"Don't go!" Felix rushed after him. "I have to get you back to Snugwarm."

Rupus snapped back towards Felix. "But I'm a wishsnatcher. I live in the coal mines. I wallow in misery. I feed on despair." Then he disappeared into the black tunnel.

"No, you don't! Don't give up, Rupus! You don't have to be a wishsnatcher. Hold on to hope!"

Felix clambered into the tunnel after his friend, instinctively reaching into his back pocket for the torch. But, apart from Rebecca's half-eaten bag of sweets, his pocket was empty. He didn't stand a chance at finding Rupus in the pitch-dark of the coal mines without any light.

"You have a home to get back to!" Felix shouted as loudly as he could. His words echoed down the long black tunnel. "You have a fridge packed with blackberry jam and a cupboard full of biscuits. You'll feel better after a cup of snorlicks!" he shouted. "I'VE GOT TO GET YOU BACK TO SNUGWARM!"

Felix's heart raced as he waited at the tunnel entrance for a reply. After what felt like an age, he heard a shuffling sound.

"Snugwarm?" the voice sounded from inside the tunnel. It didn't sound too far away.

"Yes," Felix cried. "Snugwarm. Your home."

There was a pause and then Rupus said, "No, I'm going back to my cave."

In desperation, Felix reached into his pocket and pulled out a Goldilocks Drop. He threw it into the tunnel.

"What's that?" Rupus asked, sounding wary.

"A sweet. You'll like it! You have a sweet tooth."

"Do I?" Rupus asked.

A few seconds later, his face emerged from the tunnel entrance. "Another one! Another sweet," Rupus demanded.

Felix rummaged in his back pocket and pulled out a handful. He held the sweets in his

open palm, like he was trying to coax an unruly horse. The wishes had been torn from Rupus's soul. He was a shell of what he had been. It was up to Felix to remind Rupus who he truly was.

Rupus emerged from the mine and grasped the sweets from Felix's open hand. He opened his fanged mouth and devoured them in a single gulp. "More!" he roared. But his voice was far from ferocious now. "That girl is back, by the way," he added, sounding more like his old self. He nodded over Felix's shoulder.

Felix turned to see Rebecca's car inching towards them. He still had the keys, but Rebecca was moving the car downhill using the handbrake. Her face was just visible as she peeped out from behind the steering wheel.

Felix beamed at her and waved madly. "It's OK!" he cried. "We're safe."

Rebecca stopped the car and rolled down the window. "But what about the invisible monster?" she asked, leaning out.

"He's tame now," Felix replied.

"I am not," Rupus said, between mouthfuls of sweets. He let out a short growl.

"That's the last one, I'm afraid," said Felix. "So, we'll need to head back to Snugwarm."

"Why?" Rupus asked, still looking suspicious.

"Because you have whole jars full of sweets in Snugwarm."

"Do I?" Rupus seemed pleased by the news.

"Yes, and hot chocolate and snorlicks too. But you probably don't remember what those are either." Felix paused. "Do you know who I am?"

"You do look familiar."

"I'm Felix Jones. I'm your last remaining wish."

Rupus's confused eyes filled with emotion as he chewed on the final Goldilocks Drop. "I'm sorry," he murmured. "I don't … I don't remember…"

"Don't worry, Rupus. I'm going to get you home." Felix felt sure that Rupus would come back to his senses if he could get him into more familiar surroundings.

"Rebecca," Felix shouted. "My monster friend and I are going to need a lift back to town."

Rebecca's eyes were as wide as teacups. *She must wonder what on earth is going on,* Felix thought. Still, there wasn't much he could do to explain. He met her gaze. "Thank you for coming back for me."

Rebecca gave a half smile. "No problem, ghost boy."

"He's not a ghost," Rupus said, but Rebecca couldn't hear a word.

"That's right," Felix concurred in hushed tones. "I'm Felix Jones. I'm real. I'm one of your wishes." Then a thought occurred to him.

He reached down and took Rupus's clawed hand. "This belongs to you," he said, placing the wish penny into Rupus's palm. The coin dissolved into Rupus's skin like snow. Felix looked into the still quite wolfish face and saw a flicker of recognition.

"Felix Jones," Rupus said. His eyes filled with wonder. "I think you might have saved my life."

23
The Safe Return of Rebecca Jones

*F*elix thought it best to get Rebecca safely home before taking Rupus back to Snugwarm. They pulled into the driveway, just before their parents were due back from work.

"Sorry about your windscreen," Felix said, as the three of them got out of the car.

"Yeah," Rebecca said. "Well, I guess these things happen."

"Oh, wo-ow." Rupus sucked in air between his teeth. "What happened to it?"

"You threw rocks at us," Felix reminded him.

"Did I *really*?" Rupus raised an eyebrow.

"Big rocks," Felix added.

"Are you talking to your monster?" Rebecca asked, looking around. "Because, yes, you did throw rocks and it was terrifying. I don't know how you're not a monster any more, but I'm very glad."

"I'll sort this," Rupus said. He pulled the wish-maintenance kit from his breast pocket and brushed his fingers over the shining instruments inside. Then he selected a little roll of silver tape and unsheathed a pair of scissors.

Felix turned his attention to Rebecca as Rupus clambered onto the car bonnet and busied himself mending the glass. He was back to his usual height now and little tufts of white hair had sprouted above his wolfish ears.

"Look after yourself," Felix told Rebecca. "And look after Mum and Dad – I mean, *your* mum and dad. Thank you again for rescuing me."

"No problem, I guess." Rebecca shrugged. "Well done for getting me home. And for going out to face that monster alone."

Felix smiled. "That's OK."

"All done!" Rupus said as he hopped down from the car bonnet to reveal an intact windscreen.

"That's amazing," Rebecca said, noticing the windscreen was fixed. "How did that happen?"

Just at that moment, Felix's parents' car rounded the corner.

"You'd better go in." Felix gave Rebecca a half-wave and stepped back onto the pavement.

"Will I see you again?" Rebecca asked. "Or do you have to move on now that you've finished all of your unfinished business?"

"Oh, I'm hanging around," Felix assured her. "I actually still have *a lot* of unfinished business."

Every single wish in Whittlestone needed fixing, including the wish that would bring Felix home.

"I'll be back," Felix told Rebecca. "Soon," he added, hoping it was true.

"See you, then, ghost boy!" Rebecca gave him a smile.

A wave of homesickness hit him

as he watched Rebecca step through the door.
"And goodbye, monster." She waved vaguely in the
direction of Rupus.

"Yes. See you *very* soon," Felix croaked as he
forced himself to turn away and begin the long walk
to Snugwarm with Rupus.

24
The Return of the Wishkeeper

An hour later, Felix had settled Rupus Beewinkle into his favourite armchair in the front room of 143 Silver Way. The trail of despair had faded and the house almost felt cosy again.

Rupus downed two mugs of snorlicks, a hot chocolate topped with twenty-three mini marshmallows, the last of the apple cake and two slices of pecan pie. By the end of his feast, he was looking considerably less wolfish. He closed his eyes briefly and Felix took the opportunity to inspect

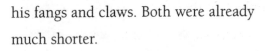

his fangs and claws. Both were already much shorter.

"Your fur is moulting," Felix told him, brushing a few hairs off his shoulder.

"Well, thank goodness for that. It sounds like I was quite the monster back there at the coal mines."

"I was scared out of my wits. I thought you were going to eat me alive."

"I'd have become a monster for ever if you hadn't saved me, Felix. Seeing you protect Rebecca brought me back to my senses. I remembered there was more to life than darkness and despair." Rupus paused. "Besides, those little bear sweets are delicious. I'd rather eat them than you any day."

Felix smiled, glad to see that
Rupus's sense of humour had returned.

"I'm sorry I lied to you, Felix."
Rupus's expression was serious again.
"I should have told you the truth about
you being a wish."

"Yes," Felix agreed. "You should
have told me as soon as we met." He
remembered the first time he'd seen
Rupus, perched on top of the penny
fountain. Felix knew in his heart that
he'd already forgiven him. "It's OK,"
he said. "I just hope there's a way
we can fix everything."

Just then, the wishofax whirred
into life. Felix fetched the message and
brought it to Rupus.

URGENT MESSAGE FROM THE COUNCIL OF THE WISHKEEPERS

Dear Felix Jones,

This morning we received a notification that a vanquisher was fired in the vicinity of Whittlestone. We have since discovered the trail of what we suspect is a live wishsnatcher in the coal mines.

Please do not leave the safety of your base. Council officials are on their way.

Yours sincerely,

Rupert Toad

Chief Protection Officer

The Council of the Wishkeepers

"Ha." Rupus smiled. "Well, it looks like they believe us at last. But I wouldn't waste any time waiting for an apology from them."

"Do you think we're safe here?" Felix asked. "Will the wishsnatcher come back and find us?"

"Oh, trust me, Felix, that creature won't be coming anywhere near Whittlestone again." Rupus shook his head. "Not after coming face to face with a real-life *wish boy*. You've scared it off for good."

"Wish boy," said Felix. "I like that. It's certainly an improvement on ghost boy."

"You know, from the moment we first spoke that day at the penny fountain, I knew in my bones that you would save Whittlestone somehow."

"Really?" Felix asked, raising an eyebrow. "I thought I was your only option."

"I suppose you were," Rupus admitted. "But that doesn't mean you weren't the best option too." He buttered some toast and handed it to Felix. "I didn't

realize it until today. I didn't realize it until that final moment when the wishsnatcher was extracting my last wish. But you've *always* been the best defence for Whittlestone, Felix."

"How do you mean?" Felix wasn't following.

"Who needs a tank full of hope, bravery and wishfulness when you have an *actual* wish boy to save you?"

Felix smiled, remembering the moment he'd snatched the final wish from the wishsnatcher's grip. It was the first time in his life that he'd felt like a hero.

"Did you really believe I could do it?" he asked.

"Oh, yes. But the most important thing was that *you* finally believed in yourself, Felix. You knew how much you were wanted. You knew you were Rebecca's bestest, best wish." Rupus smiled fondly, as if reliving the memory of the wish in his mind's eye. "No wishsnatcher could bear to be in the presence of that much hope."

The two of them sat in silence for a few minutes, reflecting on this before Felix spoke again. "Was the wishsnatcher once a wishkeeper too?"

He'd been thinking about this ever since Rupus had turned into a wishsnatcher, but for some reason he hadn't felt ready to ask the question until now.

"Yes," Rupus replied solemnly. "I do believe it was." He stared at the visible claw marks on the carpet below. "I suppose it makes a kind of sense. A creature capable of great wonders could turn into the greatest monster of all when deprived of hope."

For the briefest of moments, Felix felt a wave of something resembling pity for the monster. It was unthinkable that dear old Rupus had been a whisker away from becoming a wishsnatcher himself.

"Do you think The Council of the Wishkeepers know that the wishsnatchers used to be wishkeepers?" Felix asked.

"Oh, yes, they must do," Rupus said. "And no wonder they've kept it quiet all these years. It would cause mass panic if the wishkeeping community knew. The only thing worse than facing a wishsnatcher would be knowing that you might be turned into one yourself." He gulped down a mouthful of snorlicks. "But I'm safe now – thanks to you."

"What will happen to the wishsnatcher?" Felix asked.

"I suppose the Council will deal with it."

"Will they be able to bring it back? Make it a wishkeeper again."

Rupus's face clouded with sadness. "Let us hope so, Felix. Let us *wish* so."

25
Council Business

Soon Felix and Rupus, full of cake and exhausted from their ordeal, were asleep in a desk chair and armchair. All was still and quiet in Snugwarm that evening, except for the odd pop of the toaster or the fluttering of a wish card as it slotted through the skylight window. All the while, the dial on the wishfulness gauge was creeping up. Hope was returning to Whittlestone.

Eventually, a knock on the front door shook Felix from his slumber. He shuffled into the hallway, rubbing sleep from his eyes and nursing his shoulder wound. Two short and stout

wishkeepers, dressed in plum-coloured uniforms, were waiting at the door.

"Felix Jones?" one of them asked.

"That's me," Felix confirmed.

"My name is Glenda Bagstrop, and this is my assistant, Mr Snatt. We're here to take things forward." Glenda folded her arms and puffed out her chest. "You've obviously been through a lot with the – the, uh…"

"The wishsnatcher," Felix completed her sentence.

Glenda's nose twitched. "The *suspected* wishsnatcher. We haven't caught it yet, but the team is hot on its trail. Anyway, you're safe now."

"What will they do when they catch it?" Felix asked.

"No need for you to worry about that," Glenda replied. "That's Council business."

"But it will be OK, won't it?" Felix asked. "Will you be able to help it turn into a wishkeeper again?"

"P–p–pardon?" Glenda's eyes were wide. "How on earth do you know—" She stopped short.

Behind her, Assistant Snatt had turned pale.

"Listen, Felix," she said. "We're here to tell you that The Council of the Wishkeepers is stepping in. I'll take charge of the situation now."

"There's no need," Felix replied. "We've got everything in hand. I want to know that the wishsnatcher will be all right."

"*Suspected* wishsnatcher," Glenda said. "But, yes, we have ways of dealing with these creatures when such occasions arrive. We have every hope that if it is not restored to its original self, it will be kept safe and well, and away from anyone it could further harm."

"Now, to be clear, Felix," Glenda went on, "I'm here on the direct orders of Rupert Toad. The Council recognizes that it was a huge mistake to leave an inexperienced apprentice flying solo in this post. They apologize sincerely for everything you have been through. I am here to fill the boots, as it were."

"But there's no need. The boots are full. Rupus Beewinkle has returned to his post."

"That's right," came a voice from inside Snugwarm.

Felix turned to see Rupus, robed in his velvet dressing gown like a king. He strolled down the hallway casually, filing one of his still longer than

usual fingernails with an emery board. He brushed some stray fur from his cheek and then raised his hand in a half-wave at the two wishkeepers in the doorway. "Thank you for calling in, but I'm afraid we are very busy. As you can imagine, we have *thousands* of wishes to restore to Whittlestone. So, I'm afraid I will have to insist that you leave me and my apprentice in peace to get on with our work." Rupus smiled at the two officials while still filing his claws.

Assistant Snatt gulped, but Glenda pressed on, a little nervously, "You defeated a wishsnatcher single-handedly. Unheard of. Absolutely unheard of. But, Mr Beewinkle, I'm here on the express orders of The Council of the Wishkeepers. We have quite a few questions we need to go through with yo—"

But Rupus had already started closing the door. There was a series of clicks as he bolted it shut.

"Best to avoid getting into any of the details with them," Rupus said. "I don't want them digging through my records."

Felix nodded in agreement.

"Now, I do believe it is suppertime." Rupus spoke with such certainty that Felix felt compelled to follow him into the kitchen.

Rupus removed a couple of wish cards from the toaster and replaced them with two slices of bread. "New wishes!" he said. "*That* is a very good sign, a very good sign indeed."

"We will be able to fix the old wishes, won't we?" Felix asked, waiting for the toast to pop as Rupus busied himself fetching jam and butter from the pantry.

212

"Alas," Rupus replied. "Wishes don't quite work like that."

There was a moment of silence while Felix took Rupus's words in. It was not the reply he'd expected.

"Oh." Felix scanned Rupus's face. "But what does that mean for me? And what about the bakery and the theatre and—"

"Don't worry, don't worry," Rupus interjected. "Everything will work itself out, you'll see. All of the important wishes will come back around again." He buttered some toast and handed it to Felix. "Trust me, it won't be long before people remember all the things they had hoped and dreamed of. They'll wish again. You'll see."

Felix took the toast and set it down on the countertop. He'd lost his appetite.

"So, you're telling me we have to wait for people to wish again? How can you be so sure they will?" Felix asked, feeling deflated and confused. He couldn't see Rebecca wishing for an annoying ten-year-old brother any time soon.

Rupus met Felix's eye. Without explanation, he proceeded to down his entire cup of tea. After three huge gulps, he fished out five soggy wish cards and lined them up on the countertop. Then, with a flourish, he pulled off his hat.

Half a dozen wish cards tumbled out of his white cloud of hair. And, as if on cue, two more leaped out of the toaster with a pop.

"We'll not be waiting long," Rupus told him. "Trust me."

26
A Season of Wishkeeping

Rupus and Felix soon settled into a daily rhythm as they began to restore the wishes of Whittlestone. It was easy to feel at home somewhere as cosy as Snugwarm. Felix set up a makeshift bed with an armchair and footstool and quickly became familiar with the house layout. Of course he couldn't resist a bit of tidying up here and there, but most of his time was spent gathering wish cards and assisting Rupus as he prioritized the wishes. Wishfulness, it turned out, was infectious. The villagers of Whittlestone were wishing left, right and centre.

I wish I could buy the old, derelict house over the road and turn it into something truly magnificent.

Rupert Frightly, aged 58

I wish I was a famous opera singer.

Eva Ramasamy, aged 36

I wish for a pet. Possibly a cocker spaniel or a terrier. Possibly more than one. Ideally five or six.

Violet Renaulds, aged 82

Fufilling the wishes of Whittlestone kept Rupus and Felix busy from early morning until evening. It was only after supper that Felix had any time to himself. At which point, his mind always turned to home.

From time to time, he managed to check in on his family while out on wishkeeping duties. He'd caught a few glimpses of his dad watching TV through the front window, and he'd spotted his mum cutting the hedge in the front garden one day.

Rebecca had driven past him multiple times, giving him a double-take. Her yellow Volvo wasn't easy to miss.

As the weeks turned into months, Felix's trickle of homesickness became a great torrent that came with him wherever he went. But he tried his best to trust Rupus that the lost wishes would work themselves out in the end.

Within a matter of months, the garish *Wash & Go* signage was gone and the Blackbird Bakery's shop window was full of Regina's finest cinnamon rolls. The scaffolding came down on the Half Moon Theatre to reveal newly painted yellow walls and a *Theatre Opening Soon* banner. By mid-spring,

Whittlestone was starting to feel like the town Felix knew and loved.

Then, one day, Rupus came to Felix with a wish card in his hands. Felix gestured for him to add it to the stack, but he passed it directly to Felix instead.

"I think you'll want to read this one right away," Rupus said.

Felix peered down at the two lines of text on the card.

I wish I knew what was missing.
Rebecca Jones, aged 17

Felix nearly dropped his mug of snorlicks. This was the wish he'd been waiting for.

"I think it's time we got you home, Felix," Rupus said.

"Will you be OK without me?" Felix asked, looking around at the wish cards stacked high on

every surface. There was nothing he wanted more than to go home, but how on earth would Rupus manage without him?

"Oh, yes. I'll cope. I'm back in my stride now. And, as you know, we wishkeepers are solitary creatures. Although…" Rupus paused. "I suppose I could do with a little help now and then – maybe just on Saturdays." He smiled. "That is, of course, if you'd be willing to continue in the post?"

"Of course I would." A smile broke onto Felix's face too.

"Fantastic." Rupus rubbed his hands together. "I can assure you there will always be plenty of cake involved."

27
MEMORY MENDING

Felix and Rupus were hiding behind the hedge outside Felix's house, waiting for their moment. Right on cue, Rebecca opened the front door, carrying a plump bin bag full of rubbish. She was her usual surly self.

Felix smiled at the sight of her. Putting the bins out was her least favourite chore. As soon as she was at the end of the driveway, Felix dashed through the open door, with Rupus close behind him. The two of them made it into the front room unseen and closed the door to the hallway.

The family portrait was perched in place above

the mantelpiece. Rupus reached up and tapped on the glass. Obediently, the mother, father and daughter in the picture shuffled over to allow a grinning boy into the frame.

"Perfect," Rupus muttered as he walked back out into the hallway. He gestured for Felix to follow him as he dashed up the stairs, heading for Felix's old bedroom.

Seconds later, they were both safely inside what was now a home gym. Felix stared at the bare walls, the bulky rowing machine and the dusty treadmill. He ached to be back in the safe cocoon of his old room.

"Close your eyes, Felix," Rupus instructed. "Now, picture your bedroom as best you can."

Felix squeezed his eyes shut. He remembered the green carpet stacked with comics and his superhero bed sheets and the novelty monster wall clock his mum had given him last Christmas.

"Open them!" Rupus whispered.

Felix gazed at the brimming bookshelf, clock and neatly made bed. His room was just as he remembered it. "Wow. It's *exactly* right."

"Good." Rupus smiled. "Now, I'd better get on with the remembering magic. Memory mending is always very tricky." Rupus pulled a tiny golden needle from his wishkeeping toolkit. "Probably best if I do this bit alone, seeing as I'm invisible and you aren't."

Felix nodded.

"Meanwhile, I suggest you get yourself changed." Rupus opened the wardrobe door to reveal shelves neatly packed with jeans, jumpers and an assortment of paired shoes. "I'm assuming you don't want to do the big reunion in your pyjamas."

Felix looked down at the torn pyjamas he'd been wearing on and off for months now. "Good idea. How will I know when it's time to come down?" he asked, feeling a mix of excitement and nerves.

"Oh, I think it will be quite clear when everyone's memories have kicked in," Rupus assured him as he exited onto the landing.

Felix pulled on his favourite blue jumper and a pair of jeans. He grabbed the first pair of socks he laid his hands on from the cupboard and unballed them. They were the *Best Brother* ones Rebecca had bought for him years ago.

Felix sat on the edge of his bed and waited. He had no idea how long Rupus's magic would take to kick in.

"Pancakes in ten minutes!" came a shout from the hallway below. It was Felix's dad.

A moment later, he heard the sound of someone's footsteps tapping down the staircase. Then he jolted at the sudden sound of a glass smashing downstairs.

"Mum! Dad!" Rebecca yelled.

Felix crept onto the landing and hovered at the top of the stairs. He leaned over the bannisters to see Rebecca standing in the front room in a puddle of orange juice. She was staring at the photograph on the mantelpiece.

"What on *earth*?" Felix's dad rushed into the room followed by his mum.

"I have a brother!" Rebecca exclaimed.

"I have a son!" Felix's dad shouted.

"So do I!" Felix's mum shouted.

Felix took a few steps down the stairs and watched as his dad dashed forward and lifted the portrait of the four of them like it was a trophy.

There was a creak as Felix took another step down the stairs. All three faces turned in unison towards him, necks craned upwards and eyes wide with emotion. Felix made his way into the front room, feeling like a sailboat coming into harbour.

"He's back!" Rebecca said, looking him up and down with a grin. "Felix is home." Without a second's hesitation, she rushed to hug him.

Felix squeezed his eyes shut as his parents piled on, joining the embrace.

When he eventually opened his eyes, he noticed Rupus watching them from the other side of the front room window. The elderly wishkeeper opened the window a crack so that Felix could hear him speak.

"This is *exactly* why I never bother following guidelines," he said. "It would rule out all the best wishes." Rupus placed his hat onto his white cloud of hair and leaped onto Felix's newly wished-for bicycle. "I'm just borrowing this to get home!" he shouted as he waved goodbye.

"See you on Saturday!" Felix called after him to the surprise of his family, none of whom could see or hear the little whiskered man in the front garden.

"Who on earth are you talking to, Felix?" his mum asked.

"It's a long story. We've a lot to catch up on," Felix told them.

It was going to take a while to fill in the blanks, but they had all the time in the world. The important thing was that Felix was home where he belonged.

"Do we have any maple syrup to go with the pancakes?" he asked hopefully. "I'm afraid I've developed a bit of a sugar habit."

A Recipe for Snorlicks

A wishkeeper's hot beverage
of choice. Certain to keep you in
good cheer no matter how many
wish snags you have to solve.

Ingredients

* 1 cup of whole milk
* ½ teaspoon of instant custard powder
* 1 drop of vanilla extract (optional)
* 1 teaspoon of maple syrup
* A sprinkle of cinnamon (to top)

Instructions

1. Add the custard powder to the bottom of a pan, along with the maple syrup and vanilla extract (if using).

2. Add a splash of milk and stir until you have a paste. Then add the rest of the milk gradually, while warming on the stove. (Adult wishkeeping assistance may be required.)

3. Whisk until the ingredients are well combined and frothy.

4. Transfer to a mug and sprinkle cinnamon on top.

Notes

A good remedy for a "downcast & disheartened" mood. Add marshmallows for extra cheer.

Read on for a sneaky peek at
Rachel Chivers Khoo's next book

The Magician Next Door

Wanderdust

*W*innifred Potts eyed the glittering jar on the kitchen table. Thousands of tiny specks of Wanderdust swirled inside the glass container. Winnifred sensed the same restless excitement inside her own heart. Tonight was the night.

The magician busied herself boxing up breakables and tying down her furniture. It had been years since she'd travelled via Wanderdust, but she remembered a lot of jostling and bumps along the way.

"Wherever we go, we go together," Winnifred sang. In so many ways, she and the house were one. They were like a tortoise and its shell. Or a little white rabbit inside a magician's hat.

When Winnifred had tethered the final chair to the table, she lifted the jar of Wanderdust and loosened the lid, allowing a few glittering specks out. Adventure rippled into the air. Winnifred took a deep breath. Her rainbow eyes flashed, changing from chestnut brown to a sparkling gold. She placed the glass jar on the table and lifted the lid, allowing a steady stream of golden dust to rise up.

Winnifred stretched out her palm into the river of Wanderdust, like a small child reaching for raindrops. Tiny flecks covered her palm.

"Where are you taking us?" Winnifred asked the Wanderdust. She knew there would be no reply. She felt a lightness in her step and the sense of adventure in her heart continued to grow. Despite her great age she felt young again. "Where, oh where, are you taking us?"

Before her eyes, the stream of dust swooped downwards and escaped under the crack below the front door. Winnifred smiled and made her way to the bay window in the living room. Outside, torrents of emerald-green ivy tumbled down tree trunks. Winnifred had gazed out at the same forest view for years, but now her familiar surroundings were obscured by thousands upon thousands upon thousands of golden specks. The Wanderdust was multiplying and growing in strength by the minute. Moving a magician's house was a mighty task.

Winnifred sat down in her favourite armchair

and lifted her half-forgotten mug of nettle tea. As she sat, the armchair tottered towards the window on its creaking wooden legs, careful not to cause Winnifed to spill her tea. She patted the armrest in gratitude. *"Wherever we go, we go together,"* she repeated to herself. Who knew what view she would see tomorrow: a seascape, a rainforest, a mountaintop panorama?

Winnifred had grown attached to the forest. For years she had sipped nettle tea and gathered blackberries to turn into jam. She had rested in dappled sunlight under the canopy of leaves. But she hadn't forgotten the whole wide world waiting for her beyond the forest. *It isn't good to get too comfortable,* Winnifed thought to herself, and then she set her mug down and opened her arms wide in surrender.

"Off we go then," she said to the house. "Up and away we go!"

Acknowledgements

Firstly, a huge thank you to Annalie, who is the cleverest and kindest editor I could ever have hoped for. So many talented people at Walker Books have worked their magic on the publication process: Maia Fjord, Faith Leung, Denise Johnstone-Burt, Ed Ripley, Jill Kidson, Jo Humphreys-Davies, Kirsten Cozens and Aaliyah Riaz. And not least thank you to the amazing Rachel Sanson, whose illustrations have brought this story to life. Special thanks go to Claire Wilson. Thank you for being my Rupus Beewinkle!

This book wouldn't exist without my endlessly encouraging writers' group (aka Poppy, Bethany and

Anya). Thank you also to Mainga, Annie, Thorne, Hannah, Emily, Kimberley and Jennifer. I'm grateful to my teachers, particularly Vivienne Harron, Mr Patterson and Miss Miller. Thank you also to my tutors at Trinity College, Oxford, and also everyone at the Seamus Heaney Centre.

Mum and Dad, thank you for encouraging me to read courageously from a young age. Thank you to my sisters, Hannah and Clara, for letting me add my excess books onto their library cards. Thank you to my husband, Daniel, for always believing in me. And to our sons, who remind me every day of the wonder of seeing the world through a child's eyes.

Finally, thank you to every single person who reads this book. I hope it reminds you to wish boldly!

Author Biography

Rachel Chivers Khoo was born in Belfast. Growing up, her greatest wish was to become a published children's author. Now that wish has come true, she's planning on making more wishes … possibly involving a puppy or a lifetime's supply of cinnamon buns.

Rachel studied English Literature at Trinity College, Oxford, and Creative Writing at Queen's University, Belfast. She previously worked in book publishing and wrote her debut at her kitchen table during maternity leave.

She lives in London with her husband, two young sons and far too many books.

🐦 @rach_khoo
📷 @rachelchiverskhoo

Illustrator Biography

Rachel Sanson is a children's illustrator from the UK. Originally from a little town in the North of England, she studied illustration at the University of Lincoln.

Growing up, she wished for super powers. It hasn't happened yet but hopefully someday soon…

Her hobbies include being nocturnal, making friends with cats and hiding under large piles of blankets.

🐦 @Rachel_Sanson
📷 @rachelsansonillustration

"In my experience,
almost all wishes are possible."

Rupus Beewinkle